D
THE

THE MISSING EPISODES DOCTOR WHO THE ULTIMATE EVIL

Based on the script of the untelevised BBC series by Wally K Daly by arrangement with BBC Books, a divison of BBC Enterprises Ltd

WALLY K DALY

A TARGET BOOK
published by
the Paperback Division of
W.H. ALLEN & Co Plc

A Target Book
Published in 1989
By the Paperback Division of
W.H. Allen & Co Plc
Sekforde House, 175/9 St John Street, London EC1V 4LL

Novelisation copyright © Wally K Daly, 1989
Original script copyright © Wally K Daly, 1985
'Doctor Who' series copyright © British Broadcasting Corporation,
1985, 1989

Printed and bound in Great Britain by
Courier International Ltd, Tiptree, Essex,

ISBN 0 426 20338 0

This book is sold subject to the condition that
it shall not, by way of trade or otherwise,
be lent, re-sold, hired out or otherwise circulated
without the publisher's prior consent in
any form of binding or cover other than that in
which it is published and without a similar
condition including this condition being imposed
on the subsequent purchaser.

PROLOGUE

There is no total darkness in the universe. It would seem that Nature, abhorring a vacuum, sucks light from any source to lift the gloom.

Even here, at the very edge of the unknown that lies beyond the accepted boundaries of time and space, the tired rays of some long-dead sun, after a journey of a billion human lifetimes, gather enough strength to lift lazily the shadows on the drifting motes (of what appear to be dust), that twist and twirl in the vastness of this empty velvet wasteland in the backyard of beyond.

And these motes of dust, as if seeking further warmth, drift slowly down the dead sun's rays, looming ever larger as they approach.

Two are revealed to be meteor fragments, pitted and scarred from millennial travel. Each is over a thousand metres in circumference – simply cosmic dust, detritus of some long-gone planetary disaster that will never be recorded.

They are followed by the rusty alien husk of a burnt out re-entry rocket that somehow lost its way and never re-entered the unbreathable atmosphere of its home planet.

A few more meteor fragments also drift by, unworthy of any special mention.

Then, growing ever clearer – as if denying the rule that demands that in the wastes of space spherical is the order of the day – a tiny cuboid slowly heaves into view. A distant die that grows to be the size of a matchbox, a shoe box, a kennel to a . . .

Finally it is revealed to be what it is: a British police

box of an old-fashioned design. And like an old British policeman, it doesn't sway and twirl as the other objects were seen to do, but holds rock steady in its travels.

It is – the TARDIS.

1

Inside the TARDIS the Doctor stood stock-still at the control panel. His face was white and grim, drawn as if in a state of shock, a patina of sweat on his brow.

He leaned forward tensely to rest on his clenched fists, as if to stop his arms moving – to stop his hands flicking over the panel to confirm his worse suspicions. But it was a battle he could not win.

His right hand finally darted forward to press a button, and, with an unusually smooth hum, the outer panelling was withdrawn, and the skeleton of an inner section of the control desk was, for the first time, revealed.

An electronic maze of pulsing circuitry was on view. Pinprick lights chased each other endlessly round the arteries of fibre optic cabling. Laser-operated relays jiggled open and shut, dancing in synchronisation to some unheard inner tune. The whole of the panel pulsed with life. An electronic beast ticking over in its lair.

The Doctor stared intently into the revealed innards as if searching for some sign. None forthcoming, in seconds he had seen enough.

Once more his hand flicked out to depress the switch and the panelling closed.

He flicked another switch, and a further length of circuitry was quickly revealed. An intense stare by the Doctor, and that panelling was also closed.

Then with a low roar of suppressed rage the Doctor began maniacally pressing switch after switch.

All over the TARDIS various pieces of apparatus could be heard to hum into short-lived life as they were switched on, then instantly switched off again.

At one point the lights in the cabin flickered under the strain of the electronic load, and the TARDIS gave a shudder almost like a sigh.

Peri, who had been in the galley preparing a hot drink, rushed to see what the problem could be. She emerged hurriedly from a corridor into the cabin, then stopped and stood staring at the Doctor's manic activity with a look of utter bemusement.

The Doctor finally ceased pressing switches and stillness returned to the TARDIS. He continued to stare at the control panel, his face full of incredulous disbelief at what he had discovered.

Then he lifted his eyes to look blankly into the distance ahead, and spoke quietly to himself in a voice filled with horror.

'This is disastrous! Absolutely disastrous.'

2

On the other side of the universe, untroubled by the Doctor's apparent despair, a small planetoid floated in velvet blackness.

This object, denying the universal rule, was truly black. Light and all other electronic and magnetic waves bent around it and sped away into space leaving it invisible to the naked eye.

Indeed, if human eye could have seen this object, a highly unlikely occurrence considering its in-built ability to repel light, they would have noted something not quite right about it.

Hard to bring to mind what the problem was with this obviously inanimate object, but – not quite right. Simply – too perfect perhaps?

The deep-throated hum of a powerful motor was heard. And the barrenness of the planetoid's surface was rudely broken as a two-metre square section at its pitted centre started to sink smoothly beneath the surface, then slid away to a hidden storage space inside.

Bright light shafted out from the revealed interior, and through its intensity a highly polished slab of steel rose to fill the vacated hole.

The light silhouetted an object on the surface of the massively thick plate. It was shaped like a telescope and had a casing of glass, within which flickers of electrons danced and played. It was obviously a weapon of some sort.

The steel plate, when flush with the surface, came to a halt and the hole was sealed once more, blotting out the inner light. The hum of the motors died away and the eerie silence of space descended shroud-like.

But not for long. Another sound was soon heard, and the weapon slowly rotated on its axis, its head dipping to find its target.

A planet of twin continents appeared in the weapon's view-finder.

One continent (known to its inhabitants as Ameliera) was eternally swathed in mist.

The other was a bright green jewel of a place floating in tranquillity in a blue, blue sea. And it was to this second continent – Tranquela – that the gun was directed.

On that continent – unaware that they were in the field of an alien gun, poised hidden from sight at the brink of their atmosphere – two scientists, one male, one female, diligently worked in their underground laboratory.

Their grey hair reflected not only their age but also the amount of worrying research they had shared over the years.

The man – Ravlos – paused in the experiment that he was conducting to look to his wife Kareelya with care in his eyes. The workload they were undertaking, deep underground in the palace compound of their ruler Abatan, was a strain on both of them. Ravlos was worried for Kareelya; neither of them was getting any younger.

'Are you all right?'

Kareelya looked up, surprised at the intruding voice, but seeing the look of concern in his eyes her reply was equally gentle and given with a smile.

'I am fine, Ravlos, fine.'

'Good.'

And, satisfied, he went back to the task in hand, unaware of the nightmare that was about to befall them.

A short walk from the palace laboratory, a hillside led gently upwards to a grassy peak. On the other side of this peak a sheer cliff-face fell to blue waters that broke against jagged rocks far below.

On this grassy plateau a handsome young couple sat hand in hand enjoying the view. They were both dressed in the finery that indicated their royal status. The man was Locas, son of Abatan. And the young woman, whom he hoped soon to marry, was called Mariana.

In build and general looks she was not unlike Peri, slim and dark-haired, but her nature was calmer. Locas knew she would make a good wife.

After some moments of quietly perusing the beautiful view, Mariana turned to look at Locas, an edge of doubt clouding her face.

'Are you sure it will be safe?'

He smiled at her to ease her fear. What they had decided to do was indeed dangerous in these troubled times, but he was quietly confident that the strength of his love would be sufficient to overcome the threat.

'I am sure.'

Gently they kissed.

3

On the surface of the planetoid the tripod-based gun pulsed with a new purpose. The electrons that once drifted aimlessly, now formed themselves into a laser-thin beam stretching from the base to the nozzle, as if hungry to escape the confines of the glass barrel.

They were held in check for the moment, as inside the planetoid the final positioning of the cross-hatching, marking the field which the gun would cover, was verified on an intricate display panel.

The creature who checked the positioning was the evil Dwarf Mordant. He was chuckling to himself with pleasure at the thought of the mayhem he was about to unleash. A dribble of saliva escaped his mouth and trickled down his chin. With force of habit his tongue unrolled and licked it back into the scaly toothless hole from where it had emerged.

Meanwhile his webbed, three-fingered hands flicked over the control panel, tuning the beam and verifying the area on the planet he was about to attack.

The two eyes on stubby flexible stalks above his forehead watched screens at opposite ends of the panelling.

Occasionally, out of a lifetime's habit, he also scanned the ten crystal globes that rested in pride of place on top of the panel. Not really expecting them to shine with life – but ever hopeful. The cold yellow eye at the centre of Mordant's forehead steadfastly watched the gauge that indicated the power level achieved by the gun.

Finally, as the gauge reached maximum intensity, Mordant was satisfied.

He gave a high-pitched chuckle full of a wicked, childish glee – then pressed the button that would release the laser light to do its evil work.

The planetoid bucked as the gun fired, and Mordant shrilled a happy cry.

'Go get them, gun!'

In the laboratory Ravlos stopped working, his gentle face suddenly suffused with evil. Silently, he laid the piece of equipment he was holding down on the workbench and turned to look at his wife Kareelya, still busy near by, with loathing in his eyes.

His hand stretched out to lift up a heavy length of pipe that was lying on the bench, and he quietly crossed towards her, hefting the metal in his hand. It was obvious he was intent on clubbing her down.

He was still a short distance from her when an animal roar of fury escaped his throat. Kareelya looked up alarmed, her eyes momentarily tinged with fear as Ravlos ran towards her, ready to smash her skull with the pipe.

But before he could reach her, he was pulled up short and fell heavily to the floor. He scrabbled wildly at the heavy duty chain he found was shackled around his ankle and fastened off to the wall nearest to him. But it was no good – he could not reach her.

After her momentary fear Kareelya too had changed. From being a sweet and loving wife, she also turned into a savage snarling animal.

She grabbed the nearest implement with which she could inflict damage (in her case a sharp cutting tool) and strained to reach Ravlos. Her struggling was in vain. She too was shackled around her ankle, chained off to the opposite wall to Ravlos, and also just out of reach.

Unable to attack, they ended up facing each other at a distance of a few feet, making ferocious guttural animal noises of rage – desperate to inflict hurt, but too far apart to succeed.

*

At the same second, on the high cliff-face, Mariana looked peacefully out to sea.

Behind her Locas stealthily approached. The same look of murderous madness was in his eyes as was in the eyes of Ravlos. He was intent on killing his love.

At the last moment Mariana turned, but it was too late. Without hesitation Locas pushed her as she turned and she only had time to scream, 'No, Locas!' before she plunged over the cliffs to the rocks far below, his name echoing away on her lips.

And Locas, without remorse, simply threw back his head and howled a wild laugh.

Inside the distant planetoid the laugh was echoed by the evil Dwarf Mordant.

The terror was once more successfully unleashed.

Mordant flicked a toggle switch and the cabin was suddenly filled with the noise of the mayhem and murder that was under way on the whole of the continent of Tranquela.

And he laughed uproariously with the joy of it.

4

Inside the TARDIS the Doctor finally stopped his dashing about the cabin and ended up once more blankly staring at the control panel.

Having managed to keep out of the way and stay silent for what she considered quite long enough, Peri decided to ask the obvious. 'What is it?'

She left a pause for the reply, but as none was forthcoming, she crossed to where he stood at the panel and touched him on the shoulder to make sure she had his attention.

'What is it, Doctor? What's the matter?'

Slowly, as if in a trance, he turned to look at her. She was surprised at the lack of animation in his face, almost as though the spirit had gone out of him.

After a long pause he finally spoke dully. 'Nothing. Absolutely nothing.'

Peri was momentarily thrown by the unlikely response, then managed to voice her surprise. 'But you said it was absolutely disastrous!'

The Doctor started to pace once more, but always ending up looking at the control panel in utter disbelief.

'It is. Absolutely disastrous! The TARDIS at this moment is totally fault-free. Every piece of equipment is functioning perfectly.'

In spite of herself Peri was forced to exclaim in surprise at such an unlikely event.

'What – no faults at all?!'

'Exactly! Name any time – anywhere in the universe – and I could land you there, to the stated milli-second, within a metre of the named spot, without a hiccup of trouble along the way.'

Peri broke into a beaming smile at the thought of so unlikely an occurrence. 'But that's marvellous!'

'Marvellous! Marvellous!! You call it "marvellous"!'

The Doctor was plainly shocked at her reaction and momentarily stopped his pacing to stare at her, appalled by her lack of understanding. 'Peri - it is disastrous!'

'But why?'

Once more he started to pace as he spoke. 'Have you any conception of the hours, the years, the lifetimes I've spent trying to keep the TARDIS functioning?'

Peri managed to hide her smile at the thought of the understatement she was about to make. 'You have - perhaps - mentioned it once or twice...'

But the Doctor was too wrapped up in his dilemma to notice the sarcasm, and he talked on for his own benefit, ignoring her occasional interjections. 'The times its waywardness has brought me to the brink of disaster?'

'Well - yes...'

'The times I've cursed its sheer unruly cussedness to damnation?'

'Yes, of course I have! That's why I think it's marvellous that now it's fault-free.'

He stopped once more and looked at her coolly. 'Ask yourself one simple question Peri - what do I do now?'

The unexpected question threw her. She answered, bemused, 'Do?'

'Yes - do.'

There was a short pause as she considered the conundrum. 'I don't think I understand?'

The Doctor painfully spelt it out as if to a child. 'When we are not off on a mission - but aboard the TARDIS - what do I do?'

She thought about it momentarily, then found the obvious answer. 'You sort out the faults that won't let us get wherever you want us to go to next.'

The Doctor's face beamed at her brilliance. 'Exactly! Now I have nowhere I particularly want to go and no task to perform - and this is the time the TARDIS chooses to turn on me with this vicious display of goodness, and unwonted mechanical and electrical magnanimity. Now do you see why it is disasterous? I have nothing, at all, to do!'

She finally saw that for the Doctor the threatened inactivity could indeed be a problem – but had no difficulty whatever in coming up with the perfect solution.

'There's only one answer, Doctor.'

His face lit with hope. 'An answer?'

'Yes – you'll have to take a holiday.'

The Doctor was suitably aghast at the thought. 'What! A holiday – me?'

Peri then smiled her most winning smile. 'And me, of course – somewhere nice and peaceful – but not Majorca.'

On the continent of Tranquela, in the state room of the ruler Abatan, there were three cells placed in a row at the centre of the chamber.

The bars of the cells made an incongruous sight in such stately splendour. Even more incongruous was that in the far left cell, Abatan, renowned as peace-bringer, and dressed in his sacred robes of office, was holding the bars of the cell in an iron grip and screaming in rage and hate at the occupier of the far right-hand cell, his second-in-command, Escoval.

For his part Escoval screamed equally loudly at Abatan.

Only the empty cell at the centre of the group of three stopped them reaching each other and inflicting mortal damage, as they both fought with all their might to break the bars that divided them.

Their screams of rage were all but drowned by the ferocious battle-cries of their guards, who were chained around the room at intervals, just unable to reach each other but desperately wanting to – and to attack.

At the same moment, just a few floors below in the basement laboratory, Ravlos and Kareelya still fought against their chains, hoping to get free and kill each other.

At which point, on the distant planetoid, the gun on its tripod lost its power, and stopped lancing out its evil ray.

Inside the ship Mordant had switched the dial to zero. Now he sat back with a look of smug satisfaction on his ugly face and whispered to himself evilly, 'Don't worry, good citizens of Tranquela – soon Mordant will come to save you from the tragedy that appears to have befallen you.'

With which he started to laugh, laughing so loud and long that he finally fell off the high stool on which he perched. His laughter cut off with a shriek of fear as he found himself falling.

But the laughter didn't disappear.

An echo of his laugh was heard, followed by the chant: 'Stupid little man! Stupid little man!'

Mordant leapt to his feet and looked around for something to throw at the small abusive bird that swung in a cage in the corner of the cabin.

He picked up one of the small round globes that rested on top of the panel and threw it at the bird with all his might.

The ball hit the cage squarely, setting it swinging, bounced from the wall to the floor, and then, undamaged, bounced back up in the air.

The bird furiously squawked its anger, while Mordant screamed, equally loudly, 'Just keep quiet, right! Otherwise you're done for! Cooked, carved, and out of here for ever! Right?!'

To which the bird replied with a screech – 'Stupid little man! Stupid little man!'

At that moment one of those galactic quirks of coincidence, that perhaps go some way towards proving the theory that all life is but a gamble, took place.

The moment that the globe Mordant had thrown at the bird finally came to rest on the floor at his feet, was the same moment that the *memory* of the globe's exact copy, hidden in the TARDIS storage locker, came into the Doctor's mind.

'A what?' said Peri in reply to the Doctor's muttered word.

'A holiday ball, Peri. A holiday ball.'

'And what does that do?'

'Well,' replied the Doctor. 'Let us go and find it – and I will show you.'

5

High on the clifftop, Locas – the madness having left him – stood looking down to the cruel rocks below for any sign of his loved one, Mariana.

No sign was to be seen.

He looked to the lowering sky – tears pouring down his face. 'Mariana! I did love you! It isn't all my fault! The evil force was too strong!'

He moved back a few paces, all ready to run forward and plunge over the cliff to his death and follow his beloved, whom he had so cruelly killed, to her watery grave, then he paused. 'No. That way is too easy. No one would ever know what a treacherous deed Locas had done. I will go and confess all to my father – and let the Council do to me what my wickedness deserves. I pray that it is to be put to death.'

Meanwhile, in the state rooms of Abatan, and throughout the whole continent, sanity slowly returned. The madness having passed, Abatan had sunk exhausted to the bench inside the cell in which he had been locked.

The guards also had stopped their screaming, and leaned against the wall, or squatted on their heels at their post, exhausted, and waiting for the command to unchain.

The last to calm down was Escoval.

Having given one last shout of his hate for Abatan – he stopped, wiped his hand over his forehead as one would coming out of a trance – and then he also slowly sank exhausted on the bench in his cell.

The silence held until Escoval spoke. 'I think it has passed again.'

There was a pause, then Abatan agreed. 'It would appear so.'

When Abatan next spoke, his voice carried with it the authority of one who had ruled for a lifetime. 'Palace Guards! Free yourselves!'

As the guards removed keys from their pockets, and threw them the short distance that separated them from their fellow-guards, Abatan took a key from the deep pocket of his silken garment and threw it through the empty centre cage to Escoval, calling as he did so, 'Here!'

Escoval, having caught the key, in his turn threw a key taken from his pocket to Abatan, speaking angrily as he did so. 'You've got to do something, Abatan!'

Abatan unlocked his cell without replying.

Escoval was not intent on letting the subject go away. 'How long are you going to let the Amelierons savage us like this? This dreadful new weapon of theirs is bringing our country to its knees...'

Abatan spoke as he crossed to an ornate chair. 'We can't be sure it is the Amelierons. We can't even be sure that it is a weapon that causes this killing madness that strikes us down.'

By now Escoval was also out of his cell. He crossed to the chair of office into which Abatan tiredly sank. 'What other explanation is there?'

Abatan thought about it momentarily, but could find no suitable reply.

Escoval pressed on with his argument. 'Our people are killing each other every day, Abatan; mother kills daughter; son kills father; lover kills loved one; it *must* be the Amelierons. They've always hated our race, and now they have some dreadful new weapon that turns us into cruel animals – let us reopen the Armoury and teach them a lesson.'

The very thought of such an extreme solution stung Abatan into an angry reply. 'No! The pact made by my father's father with the Amelieron leaders has held over fifty years! I will not be the one to break it without indisputable proof!'

Escoval had seen the glimmer of a possibility of finally getting his own way. 'And when you have indisputable proof?'

Abatan paused before replying, and then gave judgement. 'Then, and only then, will I act.'

Not satisfied, Escoval decided to goad him a little. 'Meanwhile you stand idly by and let our people – the ones who cannot get to their chains – butcher each other for hours every day?'

Abatan's face immediately flushed at the reprimand, and the inherent accusation that he was not a caring leader. 'Your tone is insolent, Escoval.'

Though he didn't voice it, the look on Escoval's face suggested quite clearly that he intended to be.

Abatan was driven by this look to make a comment it would not normally have been in his nature to make. 'Do not forget you are of the "Second" family, not of the "First".'

It was now the turn of Escoval to flush with anger. This was truly a slap in the face. Abatan, seeing that he had indeed offended, attempted to take the edge off the remark with an explanation. 'I do not stand idly by. Even now, Ravlos and his good wife Kareelya, on my orders, are working on a project to discover what is causing this violence in our midst. When the cause is found, they will also try to produce an answer to it.'

'And if they discover that it *is* indeed the work of the Amelierons?'

Abatan thought about it, and came to a conclusion that saddened him. Escoval was right – the pact would then have to be broken. 'We shall reopen the Armoury – and attack.'

The look on Escoval's face indicated that nothing would please him more. Abatan noted it and decided to stress the point. 'But – until I receive positive proof – the truce holds.'

The guards, who had released themselves from their chains were standing at their posts.

As Abatan stood and, after one final glance at Escoval, walked towards the massive doors of the chamber – the guards leapt to their positions, two to open the doors, the rest to follow him.

Escoval coldly watched them go. And as the doors closed behind them, he allowed himself a wicked smile. Abatan had given him information that he would find of great use.

He spoke his thought out loud. 'So – Ravlos and Kareelya seek a solution, do they? Perhaps they can use some advice.' And with a brief bark of laughter at the thought he too headed for the chamber doors.

6

In a side corridor off the TARDIS's main chamber there was a small cupboard at floor level into which the Doctor had disappeared bodily, leaving his legs behind as the only mark of his presence.

Around him were a variety of objects that he had tossed out of the cupboard so he could more easily find what he was looking for.

Peri stood among the assorted items waiting for the next appearance of the Doctor so that she could question him. She didn't have long to wait.

Two more objects flew out, and then the Doctor emerged to inspect with interest an item he held in his hand. It was simply a square box with leads attached. He pulled one of the leads out and it unfurled – then he let it go, and it wound back into its cavity.

The Doctor seemed quite pleased and put the box down with the rest.

Before he could disappear back into the cupboard once more Peri asked her question. 'What are you doing, Doctor?'

His blank look suggested that she had better enlarge on it. 'Why all the hyperactivity in the junk cupboard?'

He was shocked at the disparaging remark. 'Junk cupboard? Junk cupboard?! This stowage locker contains some of the finest scientific ideas in the galaxy – and you call it a junk cupboard! Look at this...'

He picked up the box he had just inspected, and pulled one of its leads out. 'Attach this to any receiver...'

He then pulled a second lead out. '... And this to the

TARDIS's main control; and the TARDIS can instantly travel down the wave to the source of transmission.'

Peri was not over-impressed. 'Quite useful if one wanted to go and complain about a TV programme in person I suppose.'

Ignoring her lack of interest the Doctor picked another item, a futuristic torch-like device, from the discarded pile and switched it on; a small humming noise was heard.

As he spoke he waved it round Peri's outline. 'Or take this. Point this at the outline of any article, from planet-sized to the smallest pea. Circumscribe it. Press the second button...'

He pressed another button on the side, and with a slight whirring sound a small strip of paper was printed out from a slot in the head of the object.

The Doctor glanced at the strip. 'And there, Peri, is the exact weight, to a microgramme, of the object circumscribed.'

Having looked at the paper the Doctor crumpled it and threw it into the cupboard. 'I'd cut down on the chocolate biscuits for a while if I were you.'

She sensibly ignored the remark. 'So why – if everything in there is so brilliant – is it... just dumped in there?'

'For the same reason that if you had every kitchen aid that was patented in any one year at any patent office in the galaxy – you wouldn't find a big enough kitchen to fit them all in.'

He was about to go back into the cupboard when Peri's next question again stopped him. 'You still haven't said what the activity is all about?'

'On reflection, a brilliant idea on your part Peri – a holiday would indeed be the perfect answer.'

Peri, pleased at the thought, gave him a smile. 'Oh goody! Where?'

'That is the question to which I am trying to find the answer.'

He glanced towards the cupboard and there to one side was the item for which he had been searching.

'Ah ah!'

'Ah ah?'

'Found it.'

The Doctor took out the object, gently laid it to one side, and immediately started cramming all the other items back into the cupboard, throwing some to the very back with no care at all for their safety.

When they were all inside, with an effort he managed to get the door almost shut.

There was one item still preventing the door from closing fully. He kicked that one in to join the rest, and the door was finally closed with a slam. 'Good.'

Having watched his actions closely, Peri could not resist the comment, 'Now that's the way to treat "some of the finest scientific instruments in the galaxy".'

To which the Doctor replied equally brightly, 'If they can't stand the heat they shouldn't be in the hold.'

And with that he picked up the object he had been searching for and looked at it with interest. What the Doctor had found was a crystal ball, an exact copy of the balls that stood on the control panel in the planetoid ship of Dwarf Mordant.

7

Ravlos and Kareelya both sat exhausted. The madness having passed, their desire to kill each had also gone.

Ravlos was the first to speak. 'OK now?'

She looked to him and bravely managed a smile. 'Fine – it's passed again. We should be safe for the next few hours at least.'

Ravlos nodded his head in agreement and searched in his garment for a key. Finding it, he threw it to where she sat on the opposite side of the laboratory. In her turn she threw him the key she had taken from her pocket.

They unlocked their shackles and let them lie on the floor. Having rubbed the soreness from their ankles they crossed to the printer sitting on the workbench.

Kareelya took hold of the graph paper that was lying in reams and started to check it.

Ravlos stood at her side and touched her on the shoulder. She turned to look at him. His eyes were sad. 'For whatever happened during the madness I am sorry.'

'So am I. But we would be better off seeing what causes it, and trying to find a way of combating it, than apologising to each other about it.'

He smiled in the face of her good common sense. 'As ever – you are right.'

Then he too started checking the graph paper. Something untoward in the printout attracted his attention. He pointed the line out to Kareelya. 'Look.'

She did so – puzzled. 'What do you make of it?'

He was not sure but talked it out loud so she could share his thoughts. 'Tracings of some unknown emanation outside the spectrum that we are used to working with. Totally alien to anything that we have dealt with in our researches so far.'

Kareelya tried to contain her excitement, but this was obviously a breakthrough moment. 'Do you think it could be what we are searching for?'

Equally excited, he looked up from the graph paper. 'That is what we must discover.'

He let the graph paper fall and crossed to the electronic wave-inducer that was sitting in pride of place at the centre of the workbench. He started to adjust the controls as he spoke. 'We shall attempt to reproduce this particular wavelength – and test it to see if it *is* the one that is generating this evil among our people. If it is, we shall then try to discover where it is emanating from.'

Kareelya had crossed to the other end of the bench where a glass-domed helmet was sitting. She picked it up and started adjusting the dials on its side. 'And next time we also test the deflector?'

Ravlos worked on. 'It would do no harm. If the pattern of the attacks holds true – the next period of wave emanation will be in three hours' time. When we chain up – you put the helmet on to see if it deflects this "alien" wavelength, as it does all others.'

She paused in what she was doing to look at him, an edge of worry creeping into her voice. 'Would it not be better if you wore it – your brain is so much more valuable than mine.'

He paused in what he was doing to look at her. Even managed a smile to ease her worry.

'Kareelya, you've seen me often enough in the normal course of events go fairly "mad" when things didn't go well in the laboratory – so the sight of me going totally "killing" mad may be easier for you to bear than it is for me – who in all these years have never seen my Kareelya even lose her temper, never mind get mad at me.'

She smiled at the thought. 'Very good, Ravlos – I will test it next chaining.'

Without any warning one of the heavy wooden doors to the laboratory swung open, and Escoval entered with the sureness of one who knows he possesses great power.

Ravlos and Kareelya exchanged a glance – it was obvious from their look that Escoval was not their favourite person.

He crossed to the bench where they stood, taking in the equipment lying around at a glance, particularly the helmet still held by Kareelya.

He spoke brusquely without first having the common courtesy to exchange a greeting. 'Abatan has sent me to check how successful you have been with your researches to date. He is getting more than a little impatient with this constant madness in our midst.'

Ravlos was surprised by the remark. 'Abatan told me my findings should be for his ears only.'

Escoval's face flushed with instant anger. 'Don't be impertinent, Ravlos – you are simply a scientist, and should know that that is no way to address a member of a ruling family.'

Kareelya, having put the dome back safely on the workbench, spoke innocently enough, but knew it would sting. 'A ruler of the Second Family, that is.' And sting it did.

Even though it was true, Escoval was furious at the slight. 'You are licensed to the scientific group because you are the wife of one who, Abatan considers, is a distinguished scientist.'

Ravlos looked from Escoval to his wife, his look a warning not to go too far – this man was dangerous.

Escoval was indeed dangerous – his words spat out the threat through lips tight and pale with anger.

'It is a licence that can be revoked for impertinence, among other things. And you both know what that would mean.'

They did indeed.

They exchanged a glance, and Escoval saw the look and knew they were suitably cowed. He continued with his mission. 'Now would you both be good enough to give me the results of your researches to date, so that I can report them to Abatan.'

There was only the slightest of hesitations before Ravlos spoke.

He had sensed there could be little danger in letting Escoval know their findings to date. There was no way that a member of the Families could ever be a spy.

He indicated the workbench and the equipment there as he spoke. 'As you see we have built a range of equipment that will search out and record atmospheric and sub-electronic disturbance from any known or unknown source...'

He crossed to the graph paper and held it as he talked on, indicating the peculiarity. 'We have today isolated a new and totally alien wave-form that it would appear is spasmodically entering our atmosphere.'

He let the graph paper fall and walked back to the equipment he had been working on. 'We can't be sure that it is this "wave" that is affecting us until we have duplicated and tested it – but as the times of the outbreaks of madness and its registering on our equipment match up perfectly, it is highly likely that this is the cause.'

A look that was a strange mixture of worry and pleasure crossed Escoval's face.

'So the Amelierons have indeed created a new weapon to attempt to destroy us.'

As a scientist Kareelya knew that they had come nowhere near to proving such a thing. 'There is no way we could prove that until we have traced its emanation point...'

But Escoval was not to be deflected from his hypothesis so easily. He rudely interrupted before she could complete her thought.

'There is no need to "prove" anything. If there's a new weapon, they're the only ones who could possibly have any use for it – the Armoury will soon be reopened, and war will be declared.'

As a man of peace Ravlos was both horror-struck at

the thought and puzzled by the necessity. 'But why?'

It was Escoval's turn to be surprised. 'Why? To stop this madness of course.'

Kareelya sensed that what she was going to say would not be good news to Escoval – so she spoke it softly. 'We can do that, stop the madness, without declaring war.'

She was right to be wary. Escoval's face had grown still and cold. 'How?'

She glanced at Ravlos, wondering if she had revealed too much.

He took up the conversation. 'If it was possible to touch the evil inside men, and let it boil to the surface using a "wave" – it should be simplicity itself to neutralise the "wave" and allow goodness once more to prevail. To that end, on Kareelya's suggestion we have created a deflector mask.'

He indicated the glass helmet resting on the workbench. 'If it tests out successfully, soon there should be no need for chains.'

Kareelya rested her hand on the helmet with an air of possession, and there was a touch of pride in her voice as she spoke. 'We could manufacture enough of these, within a moon, to protect the whole population of Tranquela.'

Escoval stood stock-still at the news, almost as if in a state of shock.

Then, without a further word, he swung round, crossed to the door, and stormed out of the room slamming the door behind him.

Ravlos and Kareelya watched him go, and then looked at each other wondering if either was going to give an explanation of his strange behaviour.

As no answer was forthcoming Ravlos allowed common sense to prevail. 'We both have work to do.'

And at that they returned to their tasks.

8

Having dusted the ball the Doctor rested it on the control panel and looked at it closely. It appeared like nothing less than a perfectly round, highly polished, translucent ostrich egg.

Or as Peri had then put it. 'It looks almost like a gypsy's crystal ball, doesn't it. The sort they use to look into to see the future.'

The Doctor spoke as he picked it up. 'Probably still do. But this, Peri, is much more useful. A "holiday ball" in fact.'

'So you said – can't wait to hear about it.'

The Doctor turned the ball in his hands, looking at it closely. 'A beautifully crafted piece of work, Peri. Impossible even to see the join which must exist for its electronic innards to have been inserted.'

The Doctor continued to chat on as he viewed it. 'It was made by the somewhat unsavoury salesmen of the planet Salakan. A particularly nauseous example of the breed – one Dwarf Mordant – gave me this customised model some years back, hoping to win my aid on a project he had in mind.'

Peri then asked the question without realising the implication. 'And did you?'

The Doctor glanced over the dome of the ball in her direction. 'Did I?'

'Aid him.'

The Doctor was suitably aghast at the thought of taking baubles as bribes. 'Certainly not! As I said – a totally unsavoury race. With him being a prime specimen of unsavouriness.'

Having come across some prime specimens of unsavouriness during her travels with the Doctor, Peri wondered to herself what the Salakans' impressive unsavoury claim could be.

It was, yet again, as if the Doctor had managed to read her mind.

'Their one aim is the worthless accumulation of the wealth of any planet that a salesman of theirs descends upon. They find the planet's needs – and then fulfil them.'

Peri failed to see the problem in this. 'Well surely that can't be a bad thing. If the planet needs something, and they fulfil the need, what possible harm is there in that?'

The Doctor was about to have a minor explosion at her obvious stupidity – then he remembered that they were supposed to be in a holiday mood.

He gained such good control over his ire that he could finally manage an almost pleasant smile. 'The harm, Peri, is found in the fact that the *need* usually takes the form of the addictive...'

Peri understood immediately the possible problems, which the Doctor then went on to spell out. 'Once the whole planet is addicted, they are in bondage to the Salakans for ever.'

Her face wrinkled into disgust at the thought. 'Very unsavoury.'

'Quite,' said the Doctor, quietly. 'Add to that the fact that if no need exists – they simply create one artificially – and once more the planet is in bondage.'

'But...'

And, as the Doctor said the word, he threw the ball into the air and let it fall to the floor without attempting to catch it.

Peri, knowing that it was going to smash into a thousand pieces, closed her eyes in anticipation of the explosion, and thereby missed the fact that the ball, having bounced on the floor, shot back up again to be caught deftly by the Doctor. 'In this toy I must admit they had a potential winner.'

No smash having materialised, Peri reopened her eyes.

The Doctor bounced the ball again, caught it and then said, 'Watch.'

He turned his left palm upward, and shaped his fingers into a 'claw', resting the ball on the tips of his fingers.

After a moment there was a high-pitched musical pulse from deep within the ball, and then the Doctor's fingers slowly entered it. Still clearly visible, the ball was instantly diffused with a pulsating glow of gentle light.

As Peri saw the mix of swirling colour within the globe, her reaction was not unlike that of a child seeing snow fall for the very first time.

She squealed her delight. 'That's gorgeous!'

The Doctor was suitably pleased that she was so delighted. 'Yes – it is quite pretty isn't it. It recognises the pattern of my prints, and allows my fingers to enter, thus switching itself on and making the pretty display.'

Peri gave a start when the 'Voice' within the ball spoke for the first time. 'Good-day, Doctor – how nice of you to call upon me once more.'

'My pleasure, Ball,' the Doctor said cheerfully, totally un-thrown by the intrusion of that rich, deep and mellow voice.

'It is many time-scales since you have had need of my services.'

Just a hint of sorrow intruded into the timbre of the voice as it spoke, and the inner light of the globe that pulsed in synchronisation with the vibrations, also dimmed slightly with sadness at the Doctor's behaviour.

'It is indeed a long time, Ball. It is indeed. Holidays are not really my forte, to be honest. If it wasn't for the TARDIS turning on me in such an unseemly fashion, I wouldn't be sticking my fingers in your orifice at this very moment.'

The ball managed a gentle chuckle at the Doctor's phraseology, and it was echoed by Peri.

She stopped as she realised that now she and the

Doctor were mirrored in the ball. 'We're reflected now, Doctor – we weren't before.'

'Nothing to worry yourself with, Peri – nothing at all.'

Little understanding that it was truly very worrying indeed.

At that very moment, in Dwarf Mordant's ship, one of his ever-vigilant stalk-eyes had swivelled to take in the globe lying on the floor (where it had rolled after being thrown at the bird) and seen that there was life there.

Mordant leaped from his place at the controls and dashed over to kneel by the ball.

He picked it up gently and stroked it. As he stroked, the voices of Peri and the Doctor grew louder until finally every word could be clearly heard.

Mordant drooled with pleasure at the sight and sound.

He spoke to himself quietly. 'A long time since you've used the ball, Doctor. None of the Time Lords use the ball as often as we Salakans had hoped – but every little bit of information helps...'

And he started to laugh with the pleasure of having the Doctor on view, his laugh growing ever louder until it filled the ship and set the bird squawking once more.

'This time I will have you in my power, Doctor! This time I shall make a point of having you in my power!'

9

No laughter broke the silence in the state room of Abatan.

The Court of the Families was in session, and perhaps no sadder case had ever been before them. One of their own stood accused of murder most foul.

Locas, son of Abatan, stood, a guard on either side of him, accused by his own confession of the murder of Mariana, his betrothed.

Abatan sat at the centre in the sacred chair, from which all Family justice was dispensed. Behind him stood Escoval, his face hardly able to contain his pleasure at the discomfiture that all the other Families must be feeling at having to pass judgement on such a favourite son.

Guards stood alert at every exit.

And the gathering was completed by groups of ordinary citizens who were allowed to attend, so that it could be publicly seen that justice had indeed been done; but they had no right to vote or speak on any matter under discussion. Traditionally, only 'Family' could condemn 'Family' to death.

Abatan was the first to break the heavy silence that had fallen over the throng. His voice was full of sorrow. 'Locas, tell us how this stupidity came to happen. You know the rules. You know the chaining hours – and yet still you allowed yourself to be caught out in the open with Mariana; and then, by your own admission, brutally killed her.'

A sigh ran round the court from those late arrivals who were hearing the accusation for the first time.

The love of Mariana and Locas had reached the level of a folk-tale on the continent; all had been looking forward to the wedding.

Abatan lifted a hand for silence, which quickly fell.

'You've left a good family grieving, and brought shame on myself and the rest of the First Family; indeed, on all our Families.' A gentle agreement from all those around him.

Locas finally spoke. 'Father!' He was cut off immediately by the angry cry from Abatan. 'No! Not "father" here! I stand as one of your judges! At this moment you are not my son.'

He held the moment so that the words could sink in. And when the moment was right – continued, 'Now – speak.'

But Locas could not. It took some little while for him to get control. And when he finally did his voice faltered with emotion. 'You are right – it was a stupidity. A shared madness – but only I remain to live with the shame. When we realised how late it was, there was still enough time to get to our usual chaining place; but we also knew that the love that we had for each other was so pure, so strong, that we could never harm each other; there was no possible danger of that. So – to prove that love, we decided to stay unchained.'

There was a low rumble of voices as those attending quietly expressed their opinion of such folly.

As the noise died away Locas continued. 'Mariana's love was the purest – she felt no need to hurt me. But inside me some seed of evil was there to grow. And it grew – took over my will – and I pushed her...'

Again the excited whisper of voices filled the chamber. Locas was publicly confessing to no less than cold-blooded murder.

'No! I *had* to push her over the cliff to her death.'

With an effort he stopped himself crying at the dreadful memory. But there was no more to add.

Escoval's voice cut through the air of sympathy that Locas's tale had generated. 'This is nothing but an admission of cold-blooded murder, Abatan! He could have been chained, he *should* have been chained – but he walked free – and killed.'

Though Escoval was not greatly loved, there were still those in the crowd who agreed he had a point. He pressed his case home. 'This was no "accident" as other recent murders have been. He must be condemned as an example to all.'

While Escoval spoke, Ravlos had arrived at the back of the chamber with Kareelya. Having heard enough he pushed his way through the crowd to stand facing the Families sitting in judgement. His voice rang through the chamber. 'Condemn Locas – and you condemn us all!'

Surprise at this intrusion rippled through the room.

Though Ravlos, as a scientist, had high standing in the community, it did not give him the right to speak when the Court was in session.

The guards were about to step forward to take him in charge, when Abatan indicated with a wave of his hand that Ravlos should be allowed to speak on.

He did so with sadness in his voice.

'Locas has spoken a sad truth honestly. It would appear that a seed of evil does indeed lurk in all our hearts. We have considered ourselves civilised, pure without being pious, good men all, honest, open, ready to forgive, ready to be a friend, ready to love, and it is all a sad charade.'

This caused a ripple of comment once more to fill the chamber; however, as Ravlos continued the noise quickly died away so that all could hear what he had to say. 'The truth of the matter is – we have simply crushed down the "bad" in us. Over the last fifty years of peace, and war-free separation from our twin continent Ameliera, we have learnt only to show our good face; locked our hate and evil away in some dusty corner of our minds in the way we have locked our weapons away in our Armoury, locked them away and tried to forget they ever existed – but they did; and they do.'

From his garment he drew a section of rolled-up graph paper. He unfurled it and pointed at the line that he and Kareelya had discovered earlier. 'Someone, somewhere, has now discovered the key to our cupboard of deep-buried badness, and lets our hate out to play once in a while.'

He paused to allow the message to sink home. Then spoke quietly, indicating the graph. 'Kareelya and I have proof.'

This was dynamite news indeed; an unknown enemy was allegedly manipulating the mind of the planet.

Ravlos waited for the hum of noise to die away and then continued. 'This evidence that we have proves that Locas is no more guilty of murder than any other of the accidental murderers who have been allowed to walk free from this Court of the Families. He is simply guilty of believing that total good can exist.'

There was a pause before Ravlos gave his final judgement on all their weakness.

'Sadly – he is wrong. It cannot.'

The fact – which did not escape Escoval – was that Ravlos was winning the day, and quickly he tried to repair the damage.

He crossed the chamber to face him, a sneer in his every phrase. 'Fine words, Ravlos – but they don't bring a dead Mariana back to her grieving family.'

There was sorrow once more in the voice of Ravlos. 'Nothing *could* bring her back, Escoval. But that doesn't mean they would like the head of Locas on a salver to ease their hurt.'

As the crowd commented on the truth of this thought, Ravlos faced up to Escoval's cold stare. He knew he had made a bad enemy, and that finally there might well be a high price to be paid. Then he turned and made his way back through the crowd to stand once more beside Kareelya.

Abatan stood, ready to speak again, and all discussion started to fade away. 'It is time for the judgement. I shall take no part in the voting.'

A hush fell over the crowd: a life now hung in the balance. 'How vote the Families; first those who would condemn?'

There was no hesitation on the part of Escoval; his arm was up ramrod straight, his fingers curled into a fist in the accepted manner.

But he was the only one who voted that Locas should die.

The words of Ravlos had hit home hard.

Abatan paused, so that anybody who wished could change his mind.

Enough time having passed, he put the final half of the question. 'Those who would vote to forgive?'

There was a pause, then one by one the other members of the Council of Families put up their hands, their fingers pointing straight upwards.

They had decided that Locas's life was to be spared.

Ravlos and Kareelya exchanged a pleased glance. Whoever was responsible for the madness in their midst in this instance had been cheated of their victim.

The vote having been taken Abatan waved away the guards who stood on either side of Locas.

As Abatan spoke they moved back to their place with the other guards in attendance.

'You are now free to leave, Locas. I suggest you leave the city for a while. Find a quiet place to think. Stay close to a chaining-place and keep out of harm.'

Locas held his ground, and spoke quietly. 'The Families forgive me, Father – but what of you?'

Abatan, his voice heavy with sorrow, gave reply. 'You are my son – my seed. I bear your burden, and your guilt.'

He let the message sink home before he uttered the final words. 'Now go.'

Locas turned and made his way through the crowd that was starting to disperse.

The Family members rose, talking in muted voices to one another.

Only Escoval stood aloof from the group, unhappy

that Locas had got off so lightly, and wondering what revenge he could bring down on the heads of Ravlos and Kareelya for publicly thwarting him.

10

The Doctor was chatting amiably to the ball.

'So – we want a holiday where peace is guaranteed, Ball. No strife, no murder, no mayhem, plus...'

He paused, deciding what would make the holiday perfect. 'But, of course – good fishing.'

At first Peri had been rather thrown to see the Doctor talking pleasantly to an apparently inanimate object held in his hand, but as it was to be her holiday too, she decided she had better join in. 'Skies of blue, high sunshine level, good swimming, but not Majorca.'

The Doctor lifted a quizzical eyebrow. 'Not Majorca?'

'Anywhere but.'

'Right – there you have it, Ball; what do you have in mind for us?'

With which the ball lost its swirling pattern of colour and, to Peri's further delight, within its orb appeared a moving picture travelogue of a blue and luxurious holiday beach with people sunbathing, happily playing, and splashing in the sea, while the voice of the ball mellifluously filled in the background detail of the scene on view.

'There is only one planet in my memory bank guaranteeing peace and innocent pleasure at the stated level. A planet containing two races, each on their own continent, who have separated their cultures totally, and have not communicated for the last fifty of their planet years, thereby removing much strife...'

Dwarf Mordant had been watching the unfolding happenings on the TARDIS quite happily.

He had placed his copy of the ball on the control panel close at hand, so he could sit with his feet up on the desk and spy on the Doctor and Peri at his leisure, but the ball's next words made him sit bolt upright in his chair. 'The closed continent is called Ameliera, and very little is known of it – but the continent which I am going to suggest for your holiday...'

Mordant had finally realised what the ball was going to suggest, but its next words were drowned by the force of Mordant's furious scream. 'No! Not here you stupid ball! Don't suggest Tranquela! I'm doing business here setting up a deal. I don't want a Time Lord nosing into my affairs. That's why we gave them all a present of a ball each in the first place – so we could keep track of where they were going and avoid them! Now you're telling him to come here?! Shut up! Shut up! Shut up!'

Mordant stopped his screaming momentarily.

On screen the Doctor spoke once more. 'And the name of this Arcadian continent of sunshine and permanent peace, Ball?'

'Tranquela,' came the reply.

One huge scream of anger came from Mordant as the Doctor turned to speak to Peri. 'But of course! I should have guessed by the description! Tranquela is the homeland of my good friend Ravlos. Years since I've seen him. The ball's right – just the place for a quiet holiday.'

Furious beyond measure, Mordant nimbly leaped on to the control panel and kicked the ball hard, sending it bouncing to a far corner of the cabin, but it soon came bounding back again, via the parrot's cage, and caught Mordant a hard blow on the forehead, before bouncing off once more. The bird, being dragged from its sleep by the blow against the cage, started squawking once more.

On the TARDIS the Doctor was totally unaware that at that very moment Mordant was again chasing the ball, with the Doctor's face still at the centre, all around the cabin of his ship, kicking it furiously every time it came to rest.

The Doctor was also unaware that, when he finally removed his fingers from the ball, and it once more lost its inner light and looked as though it had ceased to function, it worked on in Mordant's ship.

The ball had now been irrevocably switched on, and while in the TARDIS it could follow the Doctor's and Peri's every move. Without being aware of it – they now had a spy on board.

'So who's this Ravlos?'

As the Doctor set the co-ordinates for their destination, he chatted on cheerily enough in reply to Peri's question. 'A scientist and sage of great antiquity. His wife Kareelya also happens to make the best "Sucksos" I've ever tasted.'

'Sucksos?'

'A sort of cross between a scone and a chocolate biscuit, which with your present weight I'd strongly suggest you keep away from, Peri.'

She was suitably offended at the slight – it was the second time her weight had come up for discussion that day, in fact.

'Will you stop going on about my weight, Doctor! I'm the perfect weight for my height – I've never felt lighter.'

'You forget,' he retorted cheerily, 'the TARDIS is working perfectly at the moment...'

'What difference does that make to how I feel?'

The Doctor turned and smiled a wicked little smile at her before speaking. 'I've inserted a five per cent decrease in gravity to take the weight off my feet.'

She made a 'Grrr' of annoyance at being caught out in such a way, then tried to hit back with a little sarcasm. 'You certainly know how to make a girl feel good, don't you.'

The Doctor was suitably aghast at the thought. 'I certainly do not!'

Having set the controls to the right co-ordinates, the

Doctor switched on the main thrust unit, and the TARDIS roared with life.

The Doctor, obviously pleased at the sweet sound it made, announced the destination out loud. 'To the continent of Tranquela, and peace, perfect peace.'

Mordant, having calmed fractionally, was once more perched at the control panel of his ship.

The viewing ball, the assault on it being temporarily finished, was again in front of him.

The 'scene', that moment taking place inside the TARDIS, was viewed in the ball as if in a round television screen.

Mordant peered at the Doctor malevolently. 'Right, meddlesome Doctor – having let me have the details of your exact landing site – let us make sure that you have a good reception when you arrive there. A welcome that ensures you don't come back here again in a hurry – if you're still capable of going anywhere, that is.'

And with that he started to set the cross-hatching on the control screen in front of him; pressed the button that made the telescope gun rise to the surface of the planetoid from the stowage locker where it rested, ready for use once more.

The control screen swirled and shifted as the co-ordinates were entered, and the hatching finally settled at the exact spot where the Doctor would land.

'So – you've picked a quiet stretch of beach have you, Doctor? Good – this should be fun.'

11

There was a beautiful sunny beach on the large viewer screen of the TARDIS.

The sea looked blue and inviting, the people, sprawled around sunbathing, looked golden and friendly.

Peri, standing close to the screen, took it in at a glance. 'So – this is tranquil Tranquela, is it Doctor?'

Having closed all the power systems down, the Doctor crossed to look at the screen with her. 'It most certainly is. These people you see on the screen have never known war in their lifetime. There is a system of conciliation between the two continents, Ameliera and Tranquela, that is second to none in the universe.'

Peri glanced at him, interested in the thought of a trouble-free co-existence. 'So what's the secret?'

'They never meet or communicate.'

Peri laughed at the thought of applying it to her life with the Doctor. 'We could give it a try, I suppose.'

In his turn the Doctor smiled at her, knowing they would miss each other's company.

Then he looked at the screen again and the people sprawled on the beach. 'They are in fact a people who have almost forgotten the meaning of the word aggression.'

'But they haven't forgotten the meaning of time.'

The Doctor was suitably perplexed by the remark. 'Time?'

'They're all wearing watches even though they're sunbathing.'

The Doctor was impressed with Peri's power of

perception. 'How terribly observant of you, Peri...'

She glowed gently at the unexpected praise.

'Let us go and find out why, shall we?'

The Doctor crossed to the control panel to adjust the necessary door settings.

Peri, for some reason not known even to herself, was suddenly filled with doubt. A strange premonition of disaster flitted through her mind. 'Won't they worry when you materialise the TARDIS on their beach?'

The Doctor glanced at her sharply. He seemed to sense some edge of fear in her voice, but looking at her standing quite calmly at the viewing screen he decided he must have been mistaken. 'I shouldn't think so. They did have a very advanced form of travel of their own, according to Ravlos that is. Thought balloons.'

'Thought balloons?'

'Yes. But they ceased using them after the peace pact with the Amelierons.'

Peri, distracted from her worries, tried to get to the bottom of it. 'How do you mean – thought balloons?'

The Doctor was pleased that the subject was now on safer ground. 'Totally empty spheroid, just large enough to take the passenger who's using it; climb inside; close the entrance behind you; stretch out hands and feet to touch the sides of the balloon in a figure "X"; think where you want to be – climb out again and there you are.'

Once more the child in Peri was on the surface. 'But that's fantastic!'

The Doctor was suitably unimpressed. 'Not that fantastic to a Tranquelan. They do have an amazingly advanced sense of teleportation in their make-up.'

'It's just that I've always loved the idea of flying off with a balloon; but the idea of *climbing into* a balloon and zooming off, by thought alone, is just too marvellous for words.'

The Doctor, finished at the controls, had crossed back to stand beside Peri. 'Some of them, particularly the younger ones, could actually do the same thing without even using the balloon.'

'How come?'

'Turned out the balloon was more of an aid to concentration than anything else.'

Peri remembered the Doctor's use of the words, 'used to'.

'So why did they let such an amazing skill just disappear?'

The Doctor looked at the people on the screen while he talked. 'There was a danger of the truce with Ameliera being accidentally broken. Remember – you arrive where you think. If mid-journey anybody had thought "Ameliera" that is where they would have arrived – and the chances were that fifty years of peaceful demarcation would have been destroyed at a stroke. So – it was banned.'

The Doctor, having seen what he needed to see on the screen, decided to get a move on. 'Come! The TARDIS has been in sight long enough without causing any consternation; so – let's go and say "Hello" to a few peace-loving Tranquelans, and get this holiday of ours under way.'

Once more a whisper of fear walked across Peri's mind. 'You're sure about this, Doctor? I've never known you to be so quite so nonchalant about diving in to face the locals without testing the water first.'

The Doctor had decided to ignore the message that Peri was feeding him with her eyes, 'Something is wrong here', and instead spoke cheerily. 'My, my! We are in a colourful mood with our metaphors today.'

With an effort Peri took on the Doctor's flippant mood. 'That's what the thought of a holiday does for me. You do think it's safe?'

It was obvious from his smiling face that he did think so, but he decided to voice it in any case.

'Nothing to fear whatever.'

Mordant, his finger poised over the firing button, watched the screen of the ball as the Doctor and Peri headed for the door of the TARDIS and finally out of the ball's range of vision.

Having heard the Doctor's last words clearly, he gave a little evil chuckle to himself. 'Nothing to fear whatever, Doctor? I am afraid you are wrong. You are very wrong indeed.'

Having walked out of vision on the ball, the Doctor and Peri had appeared on Mordant's main screen to be seen exiting from the TARDIS.

The cross-hatching on that screen was covering the people lounging in the vicinity. Their faces were clearly visible. One of them was Locas's.

Locas was not too immersed in his own thoughts to be unaware of the TARDIS appearing on the beach, but his heart was still too laden with remorse to do anything but register its presence.

This quickly changed.

The Doctor and Peri stepped from the doors of the TARDIS, into the sunlight and on to the beach.

Locas, leaning on his elbows, looked in that direction and saw them, or rather saw Peri. She had the sun behind her, and it was shining in Locas's eyes which did perhaps explain the mistake.

One word, spoken with wonder, escaped his lips as he quickly sat up straight. 'Mariana!'

12

Mordant watched the screen with interest as the Doctor waved a friendly greeting to those people nearest; in the fashion of their race they happily waved back.

This innocent friendliness was the goad that reminded Mordant of his evil intent. 'Enough of this. Time for terror.'

With which, the button was pressed and the gun poised laser-sharp above, all ready to fire, unleashed its deadly load of hate-inducing waves directly on to the beach.

The Doctor and Peri were still some distance from the nearest people on the beach when the rays of the hate gun hit them where they lounged.

Instantly the look on their faces changed from an open friendly greeting to an expression of hate and hostility.

The Doctor stopped in his tracks with such speed that Peri, close behind, bumped into him and also stopped. 'What is it, Doctor?'

The Doctor's voice was full of tension as he spoke. 'I don't know. And I don't like it.'

Peri's eyesight and knowledge of body language was not as acute as the Doctor's, so she was somewhat surprised by his tone. 'I can't see anything wrong.'

And the Doctor then realised what it was. 'Look at their faces, Peri. It is as if their personalities are changing before our very eyes.'

The people on the beach were now slowly rising to their feet, standing and looking with utter loathing in the direction of Peri and the Doctor.

Locas was among those who stood.

He had fought the impulse to stand but lost.

He now hated these strangers who had appeared on the beach; how dare they intrude on this sunny day. How dare that woman look like his beloved Mariana.

They must be... killed.

With that he started looking for the largest rock he could find.

Soon, following Locas's example, all the people had rocks in their hands and, without a word being spoken, they crossed to stand in a half-circle facing the Doctor and Peri, who had not moved on any further but simply stood waiting to see how events developed.

One of the people started a long, low animal howl, that grew as he continued.

The noise, an ancient battle-cry unheard for generations, was slowly taken up by the rest.

It was growing to a climax as the Doctor spoke, strangely pleasantly considering the circumstances. 'I hate to admit I'm wrong, Peri – but I do think in this case I've been very wrong indeed. I don't think they are in a terribly welcoming mood just at the moment. Are you ready to run?'

Peri bit down her fear and tried to keep the tone of her voice as light as the Doctor's. 'Race you to the TARDIS. Last one there is a cissy.'

The Doctor replied ominously, 'I have an awful feeling that it's more likely that the last one there is dead.'

The howling of the crowd was about to reach its zenith when the Doctor gave the word. 'Run!!'

And with that word he and Peri turned and ran for the safety of the TARDIS.

The people immediately stopped their cry and dashed as one after them, Locas leading the way. The Doctor was slightly in front of Peri and did not see that one of the people following had paused momentarily to fling the rock he carried.

High into the air it flew before plummeting into the path of Peri who ran into it, catching herself a sickening blow on the forehead.

She was instantly downed.

The Doctor, believing she was at his side, headed at speed for the TARDIS, and was almost through the doors before he realised that she was missing. He muttered her name and turned to look for her.

The people had stopped chasing the Doctor, and they simply circled Peri who lay semiconscious on the beach.

The rocks they held in their hands were held high, and over her.

Peri was about to be brutally stoned to death.

In a flash the Doctor had a possible answer. It meant going into the TARDIS and moving it closer to the scene of the assault; so he quickly went back inside – not understanding that he was going into immense danger.

Mordant had been busy, the crystal ball was now tuned to take over the Doctor's mind.

Lying on her back on the beach, Peri opened her eyes.

All that was to be seen was a circle of hate-filled faces peering down at her, and hands held over her.

She noted that each hand was holding a heavy rock, all ready to drop on her.

Even though dazed, she knew she was about to die, and closed her eyes in anticipation of that cruel fate.

13

Inside the planetoid ship Dwarf Mordant laughed uproariously at the two screens his swivel eyes were viewing simultaneously.

On the master screen he saw the Tranquelan mob all ready to stone Peri to death – and on the ball he watched as inside the TARDIS, where the ball's replica was now also emitting a section of the hate-wave directly on to the Doctor's brain pattern.

Mordant's laughter was directed more at the Doctor, who – all thought of Peri and the necessity of rescuing her wiped from his mind by an all-consuming hate – pondered who he could really hurt.

Nobody came to mind.

Only Peri was in his thoughts, but she was already being looked after by the mob.

He decided he would set the TARDIS on course for another world where he could vent his anger on more people.

Mordant, having seen enough, shifted forward in his seat to lift the power on the hate-ray high enough to make those on the beach actually drop the rocks they held, thereby ensuring that Peri died under their weight.

Before he could do so a piercing alarm started to ring out. This could only mean one thing – somebody was entering his ship.

In one corner of the cabin a swirling vortex like a small whirlwind started to appear. Mordant let go of the firing button on the panel and dived backwards from his chair, to press a button on the cabin wall. A tiny round metal porthole immediately slid open in the wall, and Mordant dived straight into it.

Once inside, he put his finger on the button that would, if need be, instantly close the shutter behind him, and popped his head out of the hole to see what it was that had caused the alarm to ring.

The whirlwind finally stopped, and Mordant saw who stood there with his eyes closed and arms folded.

It was Escoval.

Peri waited with her eyes tightly closed for as long as she could bear the tension, then, nothing having happened, she reopened them, and was amazed by what she saw.

Rocks fell to the sand harmlessly around her as the people dropped them. Their faces, now back to their normal kindly demeanour, were totally bewildered.

With muttered apologies all the people slowly drifted back to the part of the beach they had come from, only Locas staying behind, giving Peri his hand and helping her to her feet. 'Are you all right?'

She replied angrily while brushing away the sand from the back of her thighs and mini-skirt. 'Oh sure. Great! Most natural thing in the world - the locals wanting to turn me into a rock garden, not to mention a crack on the skull. Who wouldn't be all right in the face of such a welcome?'

He replied in a voice that was full of apology. 'When it happens we can't help ourselves.'

Peri looked at him questioningly. 'We have no control over what we do at all when it hits us.'

'It?'

The question demanded explanation and he did his best to give what little information he had.

'A desire to hurt; to kill, even. It comes over us spasmodically. And when it comes - nobody is safe from its power. The strange thing is - this is the first time this has happened during a safe period.'

Peri thought to herself: 'If this is safe, how tough is

dangerous?' but instead of voicing that thought she sought further detail. 'How do you mean, "safe period"?'

'The hours that it happens, have been charted by our scientists; and providing we're chained safely inside our homes during these times – no harm comes to anybody.'

Peri was aghast at the thought. 'You chain yourselves in your homes?!'

Locas was aware that what he had said must sound very bizarre to a stranger who had not lived through the nightmare.

'Yes. During these times of madness we chain ourselves.'

Peri contemplated the thought before making her reply. 'This could turn out to be the strangest holiday I've ever had.'

14

During the conversation between Peri and Locas, Mordant spoke uncivilly to Escoval. 'How many times do I have to tell you? Call me on the transponder I gave you before teleporting in. My hearts are not what they used to be.'

While he was speaking, Mordant had climbed out of the porthole, pressed the hidden button to close it, and climbed up to perch himself once more on the seat in front of the control panel.

There was urgency in Escoval's voice. 'There was no time! Our plan is in danger. The scientists have isolated the "hate-wave", and believe they know how to neutralise it.'

Mordant swung around in his chair to face him. 'What!'

'They have disc...'

'I heard you the first time! That cannot be allowed to happen! You hear me? That cannot be allowed!'

Mordant then slid from his seat and went to glower upwards at Escoval who towered above him. 'Go back immediately. You must destroy their equipment; that'll slow them down long enough for me to put my new plan into action.'

Escoval tipped his head to one side quizzically. 'New plan?'

'Yes – there is a visitor on your planet...'

He pointed his hand at the ball where at that moment the Doctor was juggling with the controls, setting them ready for his flight.

'He, I feel, will do very nicely to start the necessary war between Amelierons and Tranquelans.'

Escoval spoke, greedily hopeful. 'And Abatan and the

whole of the First Family will be destroyed as promised?'

Mordant smiled his most humourless smile. 'He will indeed, my good friend. And you will – as promised – be the new ruler of the whole of Tranquela.'

Mordant decided it was a good time to stress his 'honourable' intention, and his integrity in matters of business. 'And the whole of the universe, including the good Doctor, knows that the word of a Salakan trader is his bond.'

And also, he thought to himself, they are the best liars in the universe as well.

'Go now. You have work to do.'

Escoval closed his eyes before going into the trance that would allow him to teleport himself back to the palace, when Mordant's cry stopped him. 'Wait! Take this with you!'

He opened his eyes to see Mordant reaching into a container and withdrawing a thin tube, not unlike glass.

The tube had a golden hoop on its base. Mordant passed it to Escoval who handled it gingerly.

'Your forefinger goes through the loop at the base, and pressing your thumb against the side fires it.'

Escoval did as directed. 'Like that?'

He was about to press his thumb on the side when Mordant ducked out of the tube's path and under the control panel, screaming a warning, 'Not here! Don't press it while it's pointing at me!!'

Escoval was quietly pleased he'd managed to frighten Mordant.

'Does it kill?'

Mordant slowly came back into sight.

'No. It's a hypno-gun.'

'Hypno-gun?'

'Point it and fire and the person fired at behaves normally, but is totally in your control, and will do everything you say.'

It was obvious from the look on Escoval's face that the idea appealed.

'Tell them to forget your commands when they come

out of the trance; and they will forget.'

Escoval beamed the smile of a would-be tyrant. 'But that is wonderful!'

Mordant never allowed the chance to slip by of putting a little more 'bait' into any conversation with a customer. 'That's nothing. Some of the weapons I have to sell you to help in your coming war with the Amelierons (when, with my help, you are leader, that is), have to be seen to be believed. We Salakans are good and inventive craftsmen. Now go and do what has to be done.'

Escoval closed his eyes once more, and soon he was seen simply as a swirling vortex that quickly disappeared.

Mordant looked to the crystal ball where the Doctor was still plainly to be seen. 'My good Doctor, you do not know it yet but your brain pattern is already locked into a portion of my little hate-gun, so it can follow you wherever you go; now I am simply going to increase the power, and thereby turn you into a murdering animal.'

The Doctor had been gently hating without an object for his hate. Now, as Mordant increased the power on the section of the gun that penetrated the TARDIS and affected his thinking, he knew he must find someone to kill.

The Doctor realised only two people were near enough for him to do the deed quickly, and get rid of his hungry need.

Ravlos and Kareelya.

Having decided they must die he quickly set course for their palace laboratory.

Mordant zoomed in through the hidden eye of the ball and saw from the settings where the Doctor was intent on going. 'Perfect! Absolutely perfect.'

He would have been even more pleased to have seen that at that very moment, in the half-gloom of the laboratory, all the equipment was being smashed beyond redemption by some person unseen.

15

The clifftop was deserted, and peaceful. A gentle breeze wafted the grass, green with spring-time promise.

No stranger standing there would have guessed from the outward tranquillity that only recently a young woman had been pushed to a brutal death on the rocks far below, by a boyfriend crazed with some inexplicable madness.

And now that boyfriend returned – accompanied by an unsuspecting Peri.

After the long climb from the valley below Locas reached the clifftop first. He stopped when he reached the peak and looked at the vista.

Peri, who was there at his invitation, arrived very shortly afterwards gasping to catch her breath.

When she finally managed to speak her voice came out in a breathless wheeze. 'Phew! That's quite a climb.'

After looking into the middle distance for a few moments longer, her words finally registered with Locas and, his natural good manners returning, he turned to smile at her. 'But the view is worth it, I hope.'

Then, as if drawn, he slowly crossed to the cliff edge, looked down, and then sat, his legs swinging over the abyss.

He looked to where Peri stood watching him, then patted the grass beside him as an indication that she should come and join him.

With only a momentary hesitation she did so, being careful not to look down at the drop below as she took her seat.

They sat for a little while in silence, and then, Peri seeing that he was obviously dogged by a very deep sadness, decided to broach the subject. 'Do you want to tell me about it, Locas?'

He glanced at her briefly, and then away again. There was a long pause before he could bring himself to explain. 'This is the first time I've been here since...' but he couldn't bring himself to say it yet.

He paused for a short while and then approached it from a slightly different angle. 'I had a woman – Mariana – so like you in appearance that when I first saw you on the beach I thought, it must be her returned to me. And then – when the madness struck, and something inside me forced me to pick up a rock and prepare to kill you, I thought – not again. Please – not again.'

Peri didn't miss the use of the word 'again'. She felt a slight chill at the thought of what this could mean, and finally couldn't stop herself repeating it. 'Again?'

He turned to look at her once more. This time his face was resolute – he must confess all. 'Yes – again. We were to be married. So much in love. We came here often. We knew our love must be stronger than the terrible thing that is afflicting our land. We knew it couldn't touch us when we were together unchained, our love was too strong. So we decided, foolishly, to put our love to the test.'

Peri could guess the answer she would receive, but asked the question anyway. 'What happened?'

There was a long pause before Locas was able to confront the horror of what happened that day, but finally he began: 'She was standing on this cliff edge, looking out to sea, when the madness struck me. If only it had struck her as well it would have been all right; she would have turned to attack me too and we would have perhaps simply fought each other until it passed; but it didn't touch her – only me. Her love was pure; or perhaps she was simply unaffected. I was caught by it.

'I crossed to where she stood at the cliff edge... and

pushed her to her death.'

And with that, he looked at the cruel rocks far below where the sea lashed itself to a foam and, without making a sound, suddenly was engulfed by tears.

Peri could only look at him wide-eyed.

She was sitting next to a murderer, at the very spot where he had committed the deed.

The laboratory of Ravlos was wrecked beyond repair. Equipment that had taken a lifetime of work to gather together, and therefore had attained a value that was priceless, lay strewn about the empty room like so much apothecary's garbage. No item of glass remained intact, nothing metallic stood that had not been twisted out of shape.

The wave-detection equipment that had done such sterling service earlier that very day now had its front control panel kicked in, demolished beyond repair, its innards spewing out of itself like some electronic carcass.

Into the midst of this desolation, the TARDIS materialised. The door finally opened and the Doctor stepped out. But it is not the Doctor we have learned to know and love. This Doctor had a face full of evil malevolence.

He looked at the destruction around him and gave a pleased chuckle. Then he took the pocket control and pressed it. The TARDIS faded from view.

At that moment his head twitched into a posture that allowed his ears to pick up the small sound he thought he had detected.

Yes – he was right, somebody approached.

He looked for somewhere to hide, crossed to the chosen place and settled himself, and by the time the door opened and Ravlos and Kareelya entered the room he was out of view.

Ravlos was speaking as he entered. 'Well – having isolated the wave it shouldn't be too difficult to...'

But the shocked exclamation from Kareelya stopped him in mid-sentence.

It was only then that he saw the destruction of his beloved laboratory, and one hushed exclamation escaped his lips, an understatement of the horror he felt at the sight. 'Oh, no!'

Kareelya stood at his side, stock-still with the shock of it. When she finally spoke her voice too was aghast. 'Who could have done such a senseless and destructive thing?'

Ravlos was shaking his head with the dawning of a terrible thought. 'Perhaps not senseless. Perhaps someone in Tranquela doesn't want us to succeed with our research.'

Dumbly, like children going to check a broken toy, they crossed to the workbench to sift through the wreckage for anything that might have survived the attack.

So intent were they in their search that neither saw that the Doctor had risen from his hiding-place, and had clutched in each hand a long shard of glass, both lethal as daggers.

He approached them as silently as any cat, and when directly behind them he lifted both hands high in the air – and prepared to plunge the glass downwards into their exposed necks.

16

Using the incredible magnification at his disposal through a secondary facility of the hate-gun, Dwarf Mordant had been searching for a specific target, and finally his painstaking search had been rewarded.

On the screen in front of him was the clifftop, and caught in the cross-hatching of the hate-gun sight was Locas, who in his shame at his tears had stood and walked a little way away from Peri who went on sitting at the cliff edge.

Mordant muttered to himself as he kept track of Locas's pacing, but it was to Peri he referred. 'I don't know who you are, woman – but if you're with the Doctor best we have you dead and out of it.'

And with that he gently squeezed the gun's control.

As the ray washed over him, in a flash Locas's tears had gone.

His face was filled with hate.

And he was given no choice of the object of his hate. Only one person was present, so naturally that was the person he hated most in the world.

And as that person was sitting on the cliff edge, it was obvious what he must do.

He must push her to her death.

Without further thought he set off stealthily creeping in the direction of Peri, his arms stretched in front of him, to do just that.

Kareelya could not credit what she was seeing reflected in the domed helmet on the workbench in front of her and Ravlos.

Distorted by the glass, she could see an elongated manic figure who had both hands held high apparently ready to...

Before the thought could complete itself in her mind she screamed one word, 'Ravlos!' and pushed her husband hard on the shoulder to make him spin away.

At the same moment she ducked in the other direction to avoid the blow, as the Doctor plunged the daggers down with such force that he drove the shards of glass deep into the workbench. As Ravlos recovered his balance after the unexpected blow from Kareelya he saw who their attacker was, and muttered the name, amazed: 'The Doctor!'

Still with madness in his eyes, the Doctor fought to retrieve his weapons from the bench. One was too deeply buried to be freed, but the second one came out, and with a howl of rage the Doctor turned to attack Ravlos once more.

It was clear from the mad look in his eyes what he intended to do, so Ravlos shouted aloud, trying to get through to the mind behind the madness. 'Doctor! Don't you recognise me! It is your old friend Ravlos!'

A fractional pause as the true Doctor buried deep inside tried to reassert his authority over this evil body and mind; but it was no use – he knew he must kill this man.

He snarled like a ferocious animal and lifted the glass dagger high above his head all ready to slice it down and split Ravlos's head in two.

Ravlos saw there was no hope for him, and closed his eyes, ready to receive the fatal blow.

On the clifftop Peri had not even seen the danger of the coming blow.

Locas had approached so quietly, had so stealthily crept behind her, that even when he was directly behind her and ready to give her the hard push on her shoulder-blades that would send her plunging to her death – she was still unaware of his presence.

Her life was saved by a flower, a tiny blue flower that had somehow managed to take root at the very edge of the cliff where she sat.

The moment that Locas went to push her with all his might was the same moment that she chose to lean over and sniff the flower to see if it was perfumed or not.

Locas's push met with no resistance and he was sent sprawling across Peri to end up somersaulting over the cliff edge with a scream, while desperately grabbing for anything to hold on to that would stop his fall.

The weight of his body passing over Peri nearly pulled her over the cliff as well, but she managed to retain her hold, shocked and bewildered – how had such a thing come to happen?

Locas luckily had stopped his fall by grabbing a small branch a few inches down the cliff face, but it was weak and wouldn't hold him for more than a few seconds. His legs swung back and forwards over the abyss, unable to find a toe-hold.

Peri knelt at the cliff edge, leaned down to grab Locas's hand and started trying to pull him upwards. But she realised, with rising panic, that Locas, grinning madly as he gripped her hand, was not trying to help her pull him up, but was indeed trying to pull her over the edge as well.

Locas's hate was so intense that he was more concerned with killing her than with saving his own life.

17

Inside the Planetoid Dwarf Mordant watched as the crystal that had held the picture of the Doctor about to kill Ravlos suddenly went blank.

Without giving a thought to what would happen on the cliff-face, he let go of the gun's controls and leaped to grab the crystal and shake it, trying to get some life back into it, baffled at what could have happened.

Having released the firing button on the surface of the planetoid, Mordant's hate-gun sighed into silence.

What Mordant would have seen in the laboratory of Ravlos, was that at the very moment the Doctor had been about to deliver the killing blow – Kareelya, for some reason which even she couldn't fathom, had grabbed the helmet from the workbench and popped it on the Doctor's head.

The Doctor was immediately blocked off from the hate-ray that had been driving him to kill Ravlos, and was instantly his normal self once more.

He looked to where Ravlos stood, his eyes still closed in expectation of the blow that was going to end his life. Then he looked to the lethal glass dagger-like weapon in his hand, and said simply: 'Good Lord! What a to-do!'

With which Ravlos opened his eyes, took in the fact that the Doctor was now wearing the helmet and looked to Kareelya with warmth in his eyes, knowing she must be the one who had put it there. He spoke his feelings simply: 'Thank you, wife.'

At the self-same moment Peri finally managed to drag a

dazed Locas up on to the clifftop beside her.

Once the hate-ray had lost its power and stopped pouring on him Locas had let his feet scrabble for a toe-hold again.

Finally, having found one, he had also found the strength to push upwards and, with Peri's help, make the final ascent, and to end up back on the cliff edge lying beside a totally drawn and exhausted Peri.

What happened next came with such speed, and was so unexpected, that she had no time or energy to resist or protest.

Locas took her in his arms and held her close saying as he did so, 'Mariana! My lovely Mariana! You saved my life!'

There was a long pause as Peri took it in, then she released herself from his hold and sat up.

Locas also sat up and the realisation dawned that it wasn't his loved one.

Peri didn't want to say it – but finally could not stop herself. 'Sorry, Locas. I'm not Mariana. She's dead. You say you didn't mean to do it – but you killed her the same as you've just tried to kill me. And I would add it is not a very pleasant experience.'

With which she stood up and dusted herself down.

As the memory flooded back, Locas found once more he was fighting tears.

The after-effects of the Doctor's experience had hit home. Seconds after his muttered remark, having dropped the shard of glass, he suddenly felt weak at the knees. His face could be seen clearly through the glass of the mask and both Ravlos and Kareelya recognised the signs of the exhaustion that was sweeping over him.

Without exchanging a word, as one they led him to sit in a comfortable chair that had somehow escaped the general destruction.

The Doctor lifted his hands, about to remove the helmet that covered his head, but Ravlos gently stopped him. 'No. Not yet my friend. You can't be sure the beam isn't still affecting you.'

When the Doctor finally spoke, he could still be clearly heard, but there was the slightest of distortions in his voice. 'Beam? What beam? And what on earth took possession of me?'

Then he realised what it must have meant – Ravlos standing before him as if waiting to receive a mortal blow, and a lethal weapon held in his own hand.

He was shocked at the thought of what could have happened. 'Ravlos! You're all right? I didn't harm you?'

One would wonder where Ravlos got the strength of character form to react in the fashion he did. After all that he had gone through, he still managed to raise a tired smile as he replied, 'Yes – I'm all right, Doctor.'

Then suddenly he was deeply serious again, as he explained the facts of recent Tranquelan life to the Doctor. 'You have been held grip by a force that allows any "badness" within us, to override any sense of "good" we might possess.'

The Doctor was suitably disbelieving, and a spark of his former energy returned. 'What me! Badness? Impossible!'

Ravlos shook his head and continued, 'I'm sorry, but it is true.'

Kareelya, standing slightly behind Ravlos, nodded her head in agreement. 'For a short while you were turned into a demented creature, Doctor, whose only thought was to kill.'

The Doctor let out a brief whistle of surprise at the news. 'Well, I must say I find that thought very unpleasant, to say the least. Somebody must have a very twisted sense of humour indeed to be getting up to that sort of thing. I'm totally bowled over.'

He was about to scratch his head and contemplate further when he rediscovered the glass helmet covering it. 'Talking of which – exactly what function is this... er... bowl you've popped on my head, performing?'

Ravlos looked to Kareelya with a certain pride in his

eyes, and indicated that she should explain. She did so, trying to keep her own euphoria, at the fact that it obviously worked, under control.

'We have isolated the band of wavelengths into which this ray must fall, and this is an experimental deflecting apparatus, that will, we hope, block them off.'

Ravlos took up the tale with unrestrained enthusiasm. 'The good news being – as it immediately stopped the ray affecting you Doctor – it obviously works!'

The Doctor could not resist expressing the thought that popped into his mind. 'It must give a great sense of relief to the planet's goldfish then.'

And in spite of their obvious tension both Ravlos and Kareelya managed a smile at the thought.

The face of Escoval was on one of the banks of screens in Mordant's vision.

Mordant, having been thwarted by means unknown in making the Doctor kill, was still set on bringing him down, hence his call to Escoval.

'You took your time – what's the point of my fitting you with an instant transponder if you don't instantly respond?'

In the face of Mordant's ill manners Escoval's reply was still mild enough. 'I was in a meeting and a long way from my quarters.'

Mordant was not to be calmed so easily. 'Enough excuses! Get to the laboratory of Ravlos. They've somehow managed to take the Doctor out of my control – which means they now have some way of blanking out the power of the hate-gun.'

Escoval's face showed his amazement at the news. 'But that's impossible! I didn't leave one piece of equipment there intact.'

Mordant almost fell off his stool as he vented his rage. 'Stop arguing, Escoval, and go and do what I ask. If you want to rule that puny little planet of yours you'd better start jumping when I command!'

With which it was Escoval's turn to throw a tantrum.

'And if you, Mordant, want to do regular business with this "puny little planet", as you call it, you better keep a civil tongue in your head!'

Mordant was immediately at his most oily unctuous. An attempt at an apologetic smile creased his ugly face. 'Come, Escoval! Let's not lose sight of our common purpose. You want to rule – I want to trade. We're partners. Let us be friends as well, shall we?'

Escoval's very brief nod was a terse indication that a momentary truce would be declared.

Mordant went back to the main thrust of the conversation. 'You will find what is protecting this intruding Doctor?'

A cunning smile flitted across Escoval's face. 'I will do better than that.'

Mordant waited hopefully, to see what Escoval would suggest. 'Somebody has wrecked the laboratory of Ravlos at the most crucial point in his experiments. Obviously, if a stranger has appeared there, he must be the one who did it.'

Mordant clapped his three-fingered hands together gleefully. 'But of course he must! Brilliant!'

Escoval had not finished. 'He must also be an Amelieron intruder, and therefore part of the plot to bring this wickedness among us.'

More gleeful chuckles from Mordant. 'True! True!'

Finally Escoval came to the best part of his plan. 'He must, therefore, be arrested, charged, and executed.'

This time the horrendous smile of Mordant was genuine. 'I like doing business with you Escoval – you think just like a Salakan.'

Ravlos and Kareelya stood one on either side of the Doctor, holding the bowl that covered his head in a steady grip.

They were about to undertake a dangerous experiment – to remove the helmet and see whether the Doctor was still being affected by the hate wave or not.

Ravlos spoke quietly. 'Right – let's ease it off gently. If

the beam *is* still affecting you, we'll know very quickly and can instantly replace it.'

The Doctor was sure it would now be safe to remove it. As he spoke they gently started to lift it. 'I feel fine now, as it happens. I doubt whether there will be any prob—'

But before he could finish speaking the helmet had reached the crown of his head, and the wave of hate hit the Doctor once more.

He gave an animal howl of rage, and twisted out from underneath the helmet before Ravlos and Kareelya had a chance to replace it.

Mordant saw the crystal, now back on top of the control panel, leap into life once more.

On it he saw the Doctor chasing Ravlos and Kareelya around the laboratory, once more intent on killing them. His face immediately beamed with pleasure. 'Ah, good! The Doctor returns once more to entertain me.'

18

In the main palace corridor, a short distance from the laboratory, soldiers stood on guard on either side of the massive doors of the Tranquelan Armoury.

These doors had not been opened for over fifty years, since the truce with Ameliera had been signed in fact, and it was an offence punishable by death for anybody to look inside. Hence the constant guard.

While on duty the guards were chained at the ankle at a distance that did not allow them to reach each other.

Escoval rounded the corner at speed heading for the laboratory. As he passed the guards he spoke officiously. 'You two. Come with me.'

The guards exchanged a look of amazement; it was unheard of for Armoury guards to leave their post unguarded.

The elder of the two, Shankel, spoke for both of them. 'But, Sir, you know it is forbidden ever to leave the Armoury doors unguarded!'

Escoval's face clouded with anger. 'This is an emergency. A madman is loose in the laboratory of Ravlos. He and his wife could be in great danger – come.'

Once more a worried glance was exchanged, and this time unspoken agreement was reached as to what would be their response.

Again Shankel did the talking. 'Sorry, Sir, without instruction from Abatan or any other of the First Family, it would be more than our lives were worth to leave our post. Could you perhaps call at the guard room for other troops?'

Escoval was absolutely furious at their disobedience, not to mention the slight in mentioning that his family was not as powerful as the First Family.

His hand dived into his garment and pulled out the weapon he had recently been given by Mordant.

He slotted his finger into the ring of glass, pointed it at the guard who had not yet spoken, and fired.

No sound was heard, but a pinprick of light shot from the barrel, hit the man squarely between the eyes, and his face immediately lost all expression.

Shankel was amazed at this astonishing turn of events and started to protest. 'Excuse me, Sir. I don't think you should...' But it was too late. Escoval had turned and fired at him also, and he too was instantly still and expressionless.

Escoval was suitably pleased with the effectiveness of the weapon so far. All that remained was to give the instruction as to the guards' behaviour. 'You will remember nothing of what has happened here – but will simply obey what I say without question. Afterwards you will return to your duties here. You understand?'

They nodded their heads in silent zombie-like agreement. Escoval smiled with pleasure. 'Very good. Unchain and follow me.'

In moments they had exchanged keys, unchained themselves, and were following Escoval up the corridor towards the laboratory.

Having thrown Kareelya roughly to one side where she now lay in a daze, the Doctor was struggling with Ravlos on the floor.

They rolled over and over until the Doctor was finally on top, straddling Ravlos.

Ravlos's strength was rapidly fading. He squirmed, twisted and fought as long as he could to keep the Doctor's hands off his throat, but the battle was in vain.

The Doctor, who had the strength of a madman, finally had him in a vice-like grip and, fingers curling around his throat, was intent on strangling him to death.

Kareelya, meanwhile, recovered enough energy to crawl towards the length of chain bolted to the wall near where she lay. She dragged the heavy chain to where the Doctor and Ravlos fought. She tried to get the shackle around the Doctor's ankle – but he was just out of reach.

At that moment Ravlos gathered the last of his strength together, and with one mighty heave he bucked the Doctor off him on to his back on the floor, and sent him fractionally nearer to Kareelya.

The Doctor's foot was now just close enough for Kareelya to reach it. She slipped the shackle on and in a trice snapped it shut, shouting as she did so. 'To the far corner, Ravlos! Run!'

Ravlos leaped up and away from the Doctor and ran towards the corner as directed.

The Doctor gave a roar of anger at Ravlos's escape, leaped to his feet and ran furiously towards Kareelya. She nimbly ducked under his outstretched arms and ran towards the corner where Ravlos was sheltering.

With a scream of renewed fury the Doctor turned and ran wildly towards the corner where both of them now stood cowering. But the chain pulled him up short before he could reach them, and sent him reeling to the floor once more. He yanked at the shackle like a madman, trying to get it off his foot, but his struggles were to no avail.

When finally he realised this, he simply stood at the centre of the room and howled his moon-mad anger like a hungry wolf.

Behind him the door to the laboratory started to open. Shankel and the second guard, having opened the door, were standing there blankly.

The Doctor heard the noise behind him, stopped howling and turned to see who had entered. Seeing them there made *them* the new focus for his anger.

The Doctor lowered his head like a bull and charged at them with a yell.

This was the very moment that Escoval chose to step

between the two guards to see what was going on. He took the Doctor's head-butt full in his unprotected stomach. The force of the blow catapulted Escoval backwards into the corridor, and the sheer momentum of his dash carried the Doctor through the door after him. They ended up sprawling in the corridor with the Doctor on top, his full weight bearing down on Escoval.

Once in the corridor the Doctor was back to his normal self. The madness had instantly gone, and he was left totally bemused. He climbed off Escoval and knelt beside him, looking puzzled.

Escoval, once the Doctor's weight had been removed, doubled up in agony from the blow he had just received. He screamed at the guards through his pain. 'Arrest him, you fools!'

As they moved trance-like to do so, one to each side of the Doctor, he gallantly made his apologies to Escoval. 'I say, I'm awfully sorry. Can't think what on earth possessed me.'

Kareelya and Ravlos had arrived at the door, and they stared, dumbfounded at the instant change in the Doctor's demeanour. The look on their faces expressed the unspoken question. 'What has changed his mood so quickly?'

Locas and Peri walked along the beach together. The sun glowing gently down on them, and the shush of the sea on the sand on the shoreline, helped to give a sense of peace to the occasion. The recent nightmare on the cliff edge had already started to fade into the backyard of their minds.

But it had not totally gone.

When Locas asked if Peri would stay on for a few days' beach holiday, there was no hesitation in her response. 'No, it's lovely here Locas; and I really would like to stay and share your holiday with you, but I must go and find the Doctor.'

'The Doctor?'

'My travelling companion.'

She chuckled at a thought she had had, and spoke it aloud, almost for her own benefit. 'Can't wait to see the look on his face when he realises I'm almost as good a survivor as he is.'

Locas was toying with the problem of finding him. 'Did he say where he was heading?'

Peri considered the question, her brow wrinkling. 'He mentioned an old friend of his. Ravlis? Raverlos? Something like...'

But Locas interrupted happily before she could finish the thought. 'Ravlos?!'

Peri was pleased to hear it. 'That's the one.'

'Well – that explains it.'

'It?'

'The fact that they are old friends of this "Doctor". Ravlos and his wife Kareelya are old friends of just about everybody on the continent.'

'So how do I get to where they live?'

Locas saw his opportunity of getting more time in Peri's company. 'Would you like me to take you there?'

And Peri jumped at the chance. 'Yes! That would be great!'

She looked from one end to the other of the deserted beach, and then back to Locas. 'Is there a good bus service or something?'

Locas smiled at the thought. Then his smile quickly faded. 'Do you trust me?'

Peri's answering smile faded quickly. She knew her remark was going to hurt but she made it despite herself. 'Locas, that is a very strange question to ask someone you've just tried your darndest to push over the cliff edge.'

And hurt it did. His face dropped as the black memory intruded. Peri was instantly contrite. 'I'm sorry – that was uncalled for. I know it wasn't your fault, or even you, at the cliff – at least not the "you" I've come to know... and like. And yes – *this* Locas I can trust.'

A slight pause, and then his jovial mood returned. 'Put your arms around me then.'

'I beg your pardon?'

He simply lifted his arms so she could put her arms around his waist and repeated the request. 'Put your arms around me.'

She did so, tentatively. 'Like this?'

'No, tighter. I've got to pull you along with the power of my thoughts.'

She let go of him and stepped back. 'Now I remember! The Doctor said you travel by thought balloons.'

Locas laughed. 'Who needs thought balloons? Anyway - they're all locked safely away in the Armoury and are forbidden to us.'

Peri was suitably perplexed. 'So how do you manage it?'

'All we young ones travel by thought alone.'

Peri remembered the rest of the Doctor's story. 'Surely that's banned!'

Suddenly Locas's face took on the look of any schoolboy getting up to naughtiness. 'The old ones ban - and the young ones break the bans. I should imagine it's the same throughout the universe. Anyway - the only danger is thinking of the Northern continent of Ameliera while you travel. And who wants to think of those fanatics?'

'Fanatics?'

Locas went on to explain. 'History says they had a fetish for purity and cleanliness of both body and mind - not to mention the soul; that's what the wars used to be about in the olden days, trying to get our people to change their ways.'

Peri pondered momentarily. 'I guess it's the same the universe over.'

'Quite,' replied Locas, then continued cheerfully. 'But still - let's not spoil the day by talking history - just hang on tight and I'll take you visiting.'

Peri once more put her arms around him. 'Like this?'

'Even tighter,' replied Locas.

She tightened her grip.

'Terrific!' he said. 'Now close your eyes as well.'

A momentary hesitation and then she did so. There was a slight pause, and then she felt Locas kiss her gently on the nose.

She opened her eyes, surprised. 'Was that part of the procedure?'

He laughed. 'No – but I thought it would be nice.'

In her turn she too smiled. 'It was.' Then she closed her eyes again.

'Okay,' said Locas, 'let's go.'

He put his arms around her, locking her tightly to him, closed his eyes, and in a few seconds they started to shimmer, grow transparent, and then with a 'Pop' of dissipating energy, they disappeared from the beach.

The guards who held the Doctor were standing, blankly moronic, one on either side of him.

Escoval, still clutching his stomach in agony, had managed to get into a kneeling position, and with an effort slowly climbed to his feet.

The Doctor was full of apology. 'As I said – I am awfully sorry.'

Escoval was not to be placated so easily. He spoke the words through teeth clenched against the agony he was going through. 'You certainly will be, Doctor.'

The Doctor raised an eyebrow quizzically and voiced his surprise. 'You know my name?'

Escoval realised his mistake but decided the best defence was attack. 'Take him into the laboratory; I believe he may have done some damage in there.'

Now it was the turn of Ravlos and Kareelya to be surprised.

The edge of suspicion was clear in Ravlos's voice.

'How did you know there was damage in the laboratory, Escoval?'

Again Escoval was aware of suspicion. 'I would keep your peace, Ravlos – you're in enough trouble already.'

Kareelya leaped on the word. 'Trouble?'

Escoval swung his cold gaze from Ravlos to her. 'Yes –

strange things are happening in Tranquela, and you two are found in the company of a stranger.'

He let the thought sink in momentarily. 'Are you part of the Amelieron plot, perhaps?'

Ravlos's glance, which carried the unspoken warning that she should tread carefully, did not stop Kareelya speaking. 'That's ridiculous, Escoval, and you know it!'

Ignoring her, he swung round to see the guards still standing gormlessly either side of the Doctor. 'I said, into the laboratory with him!'

With that the guards led the Doctor to the laboratory door, pushing past Ravlos and Kareelya as if not seeing them.

Once through the door the speed of the change in the Doctor was again staggering. He was instantly a raving madman. Without any warning he attacked both guards with an incredible and unstoppable ferocity and within seconds they were both poleaxed lying unconscious as the Doctor turned his attention to Escoval, who had followed directly behind them.

For a second Escoval stood transfixed with surprise at the Doctor's brutality, but as the Doctor spun, with a wild roar of rage, to attack him, he dashed for the door.

But it was too late.

The Doctor moved with the quickness of a jungle beast to cut him off from his escape.

Ravlos and Kareelya watched from the doorway, open-mouthed, unaware that they too were in great danger.

Once the Doctor was done with Escoval, they would surely be the next target.

19

There was an empty side corridor just around the corner from the palace Armoury, and that was where Locas and Peri shimmered into view.

Locas opened his eyes to check that they had arrived at the right spot. They had. 'See - easy as that.'

Hearing him speak Peri also opened her eyes and looked around. 'Where are we?'

'The home palace of my father, Abatan.'

Peri's eyes widened at the word. 'Palace?'

Locas was proud of his father and it showed. 'He is head of the First Family - only fitting he should live in a palace. The Armoury is just around the corner. I thought I'd land us here so you could meet my good friend Shankel - he should be on guard duty there today.'

He led her along the corridor and around the corner to where the Armoury doors were in view. Turning the corner he stopped dead in his tracks, obviously shocked at what he saw. 'No!'

Peri could see no problem. Just two ornate, very large doors in a long empty corridor. 'So what's the problem?'

Locas's tone was aghast. 'The Armoury is unguarded!'

'Is that bad?'

As he spoke he headed along the corridor towards the doors. 'It's unheard of - something dreadful must have happened here.'

Having reached the door he turned the large handle to swing the doors open, explaining as he did so, 'We must check to make sure Shankel is not inside; that is against the law, and punishable by death. It hasn't been opened, or left unguarded, for over fifty years.'

With the force of his efforts, the doors were finally opening.

Peri had crossed to his side and was looking over his shoulder. What they saw made them both gape with amazement.

It was a vast warehouse.

As far upwards as they could see, and as far downwards into the depths falling away at their feet, was layer after layer of racking, on which weaponry of an amazing assortment was neatly stacked.

Thousands upon thousands of what must be the forbidden thought-balloons filled one shelf; rack upon rack of what appeared to be tanks, stretched endlessly away in another direction.

Rows of rockets, and missile heads, and electronic wonders of such strange shape that the mind could not even begin to comprehend their purpose.

Peri finally recovered enough from her surprise to make the comment. 'That is fantastic! I've never seen such a collection.'

Suitably awed by what he was viewing, Locas spoke almost in a whisper. 'Folklore tells us that it goes up sixteen storeys and down twenty. That's why the palace was built on the side of the mountain.'

'You mean? . . .'

'Exactly,' said Locas, guessing her thought. 'The Armoury doors lead into a cavity that has been cut out of the very centre of the mountain.'

Peri picked up an earlier word. 'You said – folklore?'

'That's right – nobody's allowed to see in here on pain of death. For fifty years since the treaty was signed with the Amelierons, these doors have never been opened.'

Peri again picked a phrase. 'You say on pain of death?'

Locas's sombre nod was reply enough.

Worried, Peri asked the obvious. 'Well, shouldn't we perhaps close the doors and stop looking?'

But it was too late for them to save themselves. Unseen by them, Abatan and a troop of guards had come around the corner and into the Armoury corridor.

Abatan had in fact stood within earshot while most of their conversation had taken place. Now he spoke gravely. 'It is too late.'

Peri and Locas spun around upon hearing him speak. One word from Locas broke the stunned silence.

'Father!'

Abatan ignored the exclamation as if it had never been made, but carried on talking sombrely. 'You have looked into the Armoury – and must stand trial before the Families.'

Peri didn't quite know what this meant but from the look on Locas's face she realised that it wasn't exactly good news. Abatan's next words confirmed it.

'Guards! Seize them.'

And rushing forward to take them roughly in hand, that is what they did.

Other guards slammed the doors closed, and Abatan with a wave indicated they should stay. 'You two – take over the duty here.'

The guards prepared to shackle themselves at their posts as Abatan once more turned his attention to Locas. 'Who is this woman?'

Locas had never seen his father holding such contained anger as he obviously now did, so he chose his words carefully. 'She is a visitor to our planet.'

Abatan closed his eyes and defeat was written on his face. Then he opened them again and spoke sadly. 'There is no way I can save your life, Locas. You have shown our Armoury to an outlander. Maybe if it had just been you – youthful stupidity and missing guards – I just might have been able to use my influence; but this makes you a traitor, and ensures the death of both of you.'

Peri looked at Locas, hopeful that his face would indicate it was all some terrible joke. But when he turned and stared at her with eyes filled with despair, she knew she was indeed going to die.

At first Mordant had been delighted that the Doctor had once more appeared on the crystal screen in his cabin. He had watched the long and bitter fight that took place as Escoval skilfully defended himself from the Doctor's frenzied attack. During it he had screamed unheard encouragement. 'Get him, Escoval! Give him what for! Remember you are a soldier like your father and grandfather before you! Smash him to smithereens!'

But he groaned with misery as the Doctor finally caught Escoval a pile-driver blow to the jaw that sent him reeling.

Escoval came to a halt still on his feet, a surprised look on his face. Then his eyes glazed over, his knees buckled, and slowly he fell, to end up lying unconscious on the floor.

Immediately the Doctor spun round looking for another target. And there were Ravlos and Kareelya conveniently available in the doorway.

The Doctor ran in that direction and, as he went through the door, he again disappeared from view on Mordant's crystal ball. The enraged creature screamed his fury as he picked the crystal up and threw it at the handiest object that would give him a suitable target.

Once more the bird's cage was sent swinging and the bird was left squawking. 'Stupid man! You stupid little man!'

Having arrived at speed in the corridor to which Ravlos and Kareelya had retreated as he approached, and having yet again lost all trace of madness, the Doctor pulled up short in front of them. He guessed from the look on their faces what had been happening.

'Ah. Had one of my little turns again, have I?'

Kareelya nodded her head in agreement. 'Afraid so, Doctor.'

Ravlos was pondering on it. 'Amazing. Only that one room seems to be affecting you; and only you being affected there. But no equipment in there is capable of working.'

Kareelya had been struck by a thought. 'It is as if you were carrying your very own personal "Hate generator".'

The Doctor clicked his fingers as the obvious answer struck him. 'But, of course! Why didn't I think of it before?'

He pointed at the helmet that Kareelya was still carrying. 'Let me have the protector, Kareelya.'

As she passed it to him Ravlos asked the question. 'What is it, Doctor? What has struck you?'

The Doctor donned the helmet as he replied, indicating with a wave of his hand that he was talking of the laboratory. 'The TARDIS is in there – but not in sight.'

Having put the helmet on, he moved tentatively back through the doorway into the laboratory, followed by Ravlos and Kareelya, who watched him somewhat warily.

This time he was unaffected. Pleased, he said the one word, 'Good.' He indicated the shackle still on his ankle. 'Do you think you could remove this now?'

Kareelya got the key from her garment and knelt to remove it. 'But of course.'

As she unlocked it the Doctor noticed the unconscious guards, and Escoval lying stunned where he had been struck down. 'Oh dear!'

He looked questioningly at Ravlos. 'Did I do that?'
'I'm afraid so, Doctor.'

Now free of his chains, the Doctor turned to Kareelya. 'It might be a good idea to lock the door.'

She nodded her agreement and crossed the room to do so. The Doctor made the TARDIS reappear, and turned to Ravlos. 'Let us enter and see if we can discover what's causing this bizarre behaviour.'

And with that they crossed to the TARDIS and entered, closely followed by Kareelya. When she was safely through the doors they closed behind her.

In the state room of Abatan, Peri and Locas were being put in the centre cell of the group of three by the guards.

Abatan watched sadly as the cell was locked. 'The Council of Families will meet before the next wave of madness is due – and your fate will then be decided. I fear their judgement may be that you both be left here, unchained, so you can carry out your own destruction.'

As he turned to leave the chamber Locas called out to him. 'Father! If there is any guilt it is mine. Let the woman go free – she didn't even know of the existence of the Armoury...'

Abatan swung round and answered angrily. 'No! You know the rules of the truce! Any Amelieron found in Tranquela can be killed without fear of any revenge or reciprocation by other Amelierons; the same with any Tranquelans found in Ameliera. In this way, and this way only, can the peace be held.'

Locas's amazement was in his voice. 'But she's not an Amelieron!'

Abatan's response was immediate and unanswerable. 'How can you know that?! You've never been there; never seen one; neither have I.'

Peri came to join Locas at the bars to defend herself heatedly. 'And neither have I. If there is a slight problem here you take my word for it – I am not an Amelieron – whatever that might be; I have never seen an Amelieron. And have no wish to see an...'

Abatan cut her off short, his voice cold with contained fury. 'But you have seen into our Armoury. And the price to be paid for that... sacrilege, is laid down in our law: death.'

He held the moment, giving them a chance to comment, but neither had an answer to this obvious truth.

When enough time had passed to be sure they were not going to reply, he headed for the door of the chamber, calling to the guards, who had quickly fallen into line behind him. 'We go to the laboratory of Ravlos, to receive what news he has before Council meets.'

Peri and Locas, alone in their cell, exchanged a glance.

Peri finally said what she thought in an age-old remark that left Locas looking totally bemused. 'This is a fine old mess you've got me into, Olly!'

Inside the TARDIS the Doctor slowly strolled around, looking intently for anything that could be causing the problem. 'Nothing out of place. Strange.'

Ravlos and Kareelya, fascinated by the interior, also wandered. Kareelya had picked up the crystal ball from where it stood on the panel. 'What's this, Doctor?'

The Doctor turned to see to what she referred. 'Nothing - just a Salakan toy; sort of talking travel brochure. When it's alive it's a mine of information.'

Kareelya was somewhat surprised with his reply. 'But it's "alive" now.'

The Doctor crossed to her side and took the globe from her to look at it closely before speaking. 'No, no. It's not alive until I allow my fingers to penetrate its interior; and even then it's totally personalised - only programmed to work for my prints.'

Kareelya was now deadly serious and intent. 'Or your brain-wave pattern perhaps?'

In the planetoid Mordant was watching the crystal intently. When Kareelya had first picked it up he had screamed with rage, 'Put it down, you meddling woman - you're going to spoil everything!'

He stayed quiet and still, as if afraid that the two faces looking intently into the crystal could see right through it into his cabin.

The face of Ravlos also came into view. As he spoke every word was clearly heard. 'What are you suggesting, Kareelya?'

Then Mordant's worst fears were realised. She had 'the power'.

'This object - though apparently dead - is alive.'

The Doctor was seen to turn to Ravlos. 'What do you think, my friend?'

Mordant shouted the remark to ease his tension.

'That's right, Doctor! Never take the word of a woman for anything.'

Kareelya held up her hand for the Doctor and Ravlos to be quiet. 'Shush!'

Then closed her eyes and concentrated intently.

Mordant immediately froze, and held his breath. He sensed what was coming – and he was right.

'There is someone or something at the other end of this receiver. I almost heard what it was saying.'

Kareelya turned to look at Ravlos as if for confirmation. 'You know my sensitivity to any wave emanation?'

He nodded his head. 'I do indeed, Kareelya. I do indeed.'

Kareelya then looked to the Doctor. 'Take my word – it is alive.'

Mordant closed his eyes in fury.

In the TARDIS the Doctor took the ball from Kareelya and looked at it closely. Then he put it down carefully on top of the control panel and spoke softly. 'What does it make you think is going on, Kareelya?'

She thought it out momentarily then replied, pacing as she spoke. 'If it was tuned to your brain-wave pattern, Doctor, it could also perhaps be used to act as a local transmitter for the hate-wave, but only affecting you.

'It also must be of a very small power – hence its working in the room, but not working in the corridor. And it could certainly be the cause of your madness.'

The Doctor picked up the globe once more, stared at it intently and spoke almost as if he were talking to Mordant, who stared back defiantly from the planetoid.

'How stupid of me not to realise it before. To take a gift from a Salakan is madness indeed. All these ages this toy has been waiting to do its work. And now – if it is doing its work and being used against me, it can only mean one thing: a Salakan salesman has business on this planet. And it's more than likely that that salesman is none other than the detestable Dwarf Mordant who gave me this present in the first place.'

20

The message had finally sunk home and Peri was suitably furious with the stupidity of Locas's father having the temerity to suggest she could be anything but a creature from Earth. And why it should matter in any case.

'But this is silly! I'm no Amelieron. You know it – I know it. And all we did was look through a stupid doorway at thousands of ray guns and rockets and planes and what have you.'

With contained fury Peri stood up from the bench where she had been sitting to stand in front of Locas and argue her point. 'Look, Locas, I don't want to stay here and get driven dotty enough to try to kill you while you're trying to kill me. Let me hang on to you in a quick cuddle, so you can travel us out of here!'

Locas even managed a fairly grim smile at the thought, before explaining the impossibility of doing what she suggested. 'My father knows that I would never do that. That's why he didn't even bother to have us guarded. I have already accidentally shamed my family's honour – and to leave now would simply be an admission of that guilt. The end of the First Family's rule would be guaranteed.'

Peri thought about it momentarily before posing her question. 'How come?'

The response was instant. 'Father would have to stand down from that place of honour, and let the family of Escoval take power.'

The way Locas spoke the name, almost as an oath, made Peri realise he was not exactly a favourite. She sat down on the bench next to him. 'Escoval?'

'Leader of the Second Family – an unpleasant person with a thirst for power.'

'Not exactly good news if he took over?'

Peri's question was really rhetorical, but Locas answered it anyway.

'It would be a disaster for the whole of the planet, not just Tranquela.'

'Why?' said Peri, interested.

Locas thought a moment before replying, then decided there was no harm in telling her. 'All know his desire to break the truce, reopen the Armoury, and go to war with Ameliera.'

'But why?'

'The Second Family have always traditionally played a great part in the managing of any war situation. It is their traditional skill. Now there has been no war for over fifty years their power has faded until it is virtually non-existent. The only way they can achieve that position of eminence again is either by becoming First Family, or by starting a war.'

He turned to look at Peri, and for the first time the look in his eyes, and the strength of obligation to a greater good in his voice, told her that she was indeed dealing with a member of a royal family. 'My father knows I would rather die than let that fate befall my people, after fifty years of hard-won peace.'

Peri spoke for her own benefit. 'So bang goes a quick cuddle; and exiting happily.'

Mordant was watching the crystal intently. The Doctor was being tied outstretched to the TARDIS control panel, his back to the controls, by Ravlos and Kareelya.

No words had been exchanged between the three of them. The Doctor had simply gone to the stowage locker and got a short length of thin but unbreakable twine, handed it to Ravlos and looked at him.

Ravlos had thought a moment, then exchanged a glance with Kareelya who had nodded her head and then spoken the only words in the exchange. 'A good idea, Doctor – and chances are it will work.'

In the planetoid ship Mordant screamed furiously. 'What will work! And why on earth don't you talk out loud like civilised people, so I can know what is going on!'

He stopped shouting as he noted Kareelya stop in her task and listen intently. A pause, and then she went back to the task of tying the Doctor.

Mordant next spoke in a whisper for his own benefit. 'I don't like this, I don't like this one bit!'

He grabbed the transponder mike and spoke into it in a harsh and ugly whisper, 'Escoval! Escoval, can you hear me! We must act now! War must be declared! The Doctor is getting too close to guessing the truth of what I plan! Escoval! Escoval!'

Inside the laboratory, the soldiers still lay unconscious, as did Escoval. But a whisper of words could be heard coming from somewhere near his ear. In fact, behind his ear-lobe, so small that it would have needed a microscope to pick it out from any other pore, was embedded the transponder receiver. This was where the voice was coming from.

'Escoval! Do you hear me. Get to the transponder now! I want to talk! Escoval, answer me!'

Escoval stirred slightly, gave a groan, and was then unconscious once more.

Abatan and his guards had marched along the corridor and reached the laboratory doors which they found closed against them.

With a nod Abatan indicated to the lead guards that the doors should be opened. The guards attempted to do so, but found they were locked.

'Knock.'

The word rang out tersely.

One guard rapped hard on the doors. The sound finally echoed away – and no response was forthcoming.

Abatan's lips were tinged white with tension. He sensed something was wrong here. A fractional pause and then the decision was made. 'Break it down.'

Inside the TARDIS, the Doctor was now firmly strapped down to the control panel.

It was an incongruous, and almost funny, sight to see him so constrained and still wearing the protective dome upon his head, but there was no trace of humour in the voice of Ravlos as he spoke. 'Are you sure about this, Doctor?'

There was no hesitation in the Doctor's voice. 'Yes – I'm sure.'

Kareelya then spoke the words of warning softly. 'It may not work.'

At which the Doctor nodded his agreement. 'True – but at least being tied down like this ensures that I will not be able to attack you and Ravlos physically when the hate strikes me.'

He managed a watery smile at the thought of the next understatement that he was about to make. 'If it doesn't work you can put the helmet straight back on me again – and nothing will be lost. But do it quickly please – it is not a pleasant sensation being riven by hate.'

Kareelya nodded sympathetically as she moved into a position where she could get hold of the helmet. 'We know the feeling well.'

Ravlos moved into a position on the other side of the Doctor, where he would be able to take hold of the helmet also. 'Very good, Doctor, if you really are sure.'

The Doctor simply nodded his head.

In unison Ravlos and Kareelya put their hands on either side of the helmet, looked at each other silently, getting the timing right. Then, as one they lifted it up and off his head.

Instantly the Doctor was back to madness, and fighting an impossible battle to escape his bonds.

His arms being held too tightly, he kicked out desperately to get a chance to hurt Kareelya and

Ravlos, making them almost drop the bowl. But they got around the Doctor's flailing body, and carefully placed the helmet over the crystal.

The Doctor's manic gyrations instantly stopped, and he fell back against the panel exhausted as the hate left him.

None of them knew that inside the ship of Mordant the crystal had gone blank – and once more it had been thrown at the cage of the long-suffering and now squawking bird, whose cage had again been sent swinging madly.

Inside the TARDIS the Doctor instantly recovered his strength and said in a pleasant understatement: 'Good. It worked. Now free me quickly – I have work to do.'

With which Ravlos and Kareelya set about doing exactly that.

Inside the laboratory, Escoval was slowly stirring back into consciousness.

The noise that was dragging him back to alertness was the muffled sound of hammering coming from the other side of the large laboratory doors. They were proving much harder to break down than the troops or Abatan had anticipated.

Escoval listened to the noise, momentarily wondering what could be going on. And then the voice of Mordant, a tiny distant hollering in his ear, registered and he gave it his full attention, straining to hear what was being said. 'Get to the transponder now!' it cried. 'Our plan is in danger of being uncovered!'

Escoval noted that the two guards lying close by him were slowly stirring into life, and also that some strange box with POLICE written on the side had appeared in the laboratory. Suddenly he had an inkling of what might be going on. This was all something to do with the Doctor that Mordant had mentioned.

With that the guard nearest him opened his eyes groggily.

By now the door was starting to give way in the face of a concerted attack, and Escoval knew what this must mean.

Abatan and his troops were on hand.

He knew what he must do to protect himself. Get the guards back under his command. He struggled unsteadily to his feet, fished in his pocket to find the hypno-gun; noted that fortunately it had not been broken in his struggle with the Doctor.

Having got it out, and hooked his finger into the trigger mechanism, he crossed to the guard who was just starting to sit up, and shot him once more square between the eyes.

The guard simply looked at him blankly, and then fell back to lie still, with his sightless eyes staring upwards.

Escoval knelt at his side and lifted his head up, whispering urgently. 'Can you hear me?'

The guard groaned an incomprehensible reply. Escoval persisted, urging him to attention, with a series of sharp slaps backwards and forwards across his face. 'Can you hear me?'

The guard struggled unsuccessfully to escape the blows, and then, alert once more, heaved himself to a sitting position, managing to speak in a dull voice as he did so. 'Yes, yes. I hear you.'

Escoval was well pleased. The tone of the man's voice told him what he needed to know.

The man was once more in his power. 'Good.'

With that Escoval pointed the hypno-gun between the guard's eyes and shot him for the second time. 'Just to be sure.' Then he spoke forcefully. 'You will agree everything I say is the absolute truth. Repeat.'

A momentary pause, then the guard responded. 'You will agree everything I say is the absolute truth.'

Escoval flushed with anger at the man's stupidity. 'No no! Just remember everything I say is the absolute truth.'

A pause, and then the reply he had hoped for. 'I will remember.'

Meanwhile, Shankel had also surfaced to consciousness. Without moving from where he lay he had been watching Escoval's treatment of his fellow-guard.

With a growing sense of outrage and fear, he had realised what was happening. The guard had been turned into a mindless zombie before his eyes.

Shankel had managed to stagger to his feet. Though his head was swimming, he set off, slowly creeping towards Escoval where he crouched over the guard.

He was almost upon him when a shard of glass that he hadn't seen crunched under his foot.

Escoval spun round at the noise and saw Shankel.

Shankel suddenly thought better of attacking him – after all he was a member of the Families – and instead ran for the laboratory doors hoping to get them open and let his fellow-guards in.

But as he reached the door Escoval fired, hitting him in the back of the neck.

He spun around to face Escoval, and the next shot scored a hit right between his eyes. He was left standing at the door, which had finally crumbled open behind him.

Escoval screamed his command against the noise of the falling door. 'You will agree! Everything I say is the absolute truth!!'

And with that, as Shankel nodded his head in unspoken agreement, the door opened behind him and thrust him to one side.

By the time the door was fully open, Escoval was back lying on the floor pretending to be semiconscious, the hypnotised guard nearest to him looking down at him dully.

The doors having opened the guards with Abatan immediately took Shankel prisoner, holding him tight, while others crossed to do likewise to the guard looking down on Escoval.

Abatan, seeing Escoval lying there, quickly crossed to him and knelt beside him, lifting his head and speaking loudly enough to override his apparent unconsciousness.

'Escoval. Escoval.'

Slowly, Escoval's eyes flickered open with the feigned returning of his senses.

Abatan urgently continued his questioning. 'What happened here?'

But Escoval was in no hurry to reply. In fact he was secretly rather enjoying the game, knowing that he had the hypnotised guards in his power.

Finally he sat up, as if suddenly coming to his full senses.

He looked at the TARDIS, then turned to speak earnestly to Abatan. 'We must stop them!'

Abatan was suitably perplexed. 'Stop who?'

Escoval dropped the bombshell. 'Ravlos and Kareelya!'

He was not to be disappointed. Abatan reacted with the expected cry of amazement. 'What?!'

And then Escoval's lying was in full flood. 'They smashed all the equipment so we couldn't trace the source of the hate ray. I found them doing it – ran to get these guards from the Armoury, and when we came back, there was an Amelieron here with them, he attacked all three of us and then...'

His wave indicated the TARDIS. 'They climbed into that Amelieron ship – and for all I know they're still in there.'

Abatan crossed to Shankel where he stood dumbly at the door. He knew Shankel well through his friendship with his son Locas, and knew him as an honourable and honest young man.

He spoke the question softly. 'Is this true?'

A pause, so long it felt to Escoval that his heart would stop beating any second with the tension of the moment.

He should not have worried. The Dwarf had given him a powerful weapon indeed.

Shankel finally nodded an unspoken, 'Yes.'

But that was not good enough for Abatan, he wanted to hear the words for himself. He repeated the question more forcefully. 'I ask if this thing that Escoval tells me is true?!'

The guard simply stared at him blankly.

'Answer me! Or suffer the consequences for such disobedience!'

Finally, again much to the relief of Escoval, Shankel spoke. His sentences clipped, and his words monosyllabic, but clearly understandable, confirmed the lie. 'Yes. It is true. We left the Armoury unguarded. Came here with Escoval. Ravlos and Kareelya were smashing equipment. An Amelieron was here with them – attacked us. Then they went into . . .' Then he pointed at the TARDIS, not having any word to describe it but the one planted by Escoval. '. . . the Amelieron ship.'

Abatan looked thoughtfully at Shankel for a moment. He was of a mind that something was not right, but had no way of being able to say what it was. Finally he decided what was the correct course of action. 'Take both these guards to the cells. They must face Council for this breach of duty. There is *no* excuse for leaving the Armoury unguarded, not even Amelieron intruders.'

And as they were led away Escoval gloated at Abatan's choice of words. He had obviously accepted Escoval's story, hook, line and sinker.

With luck, war with Ameliera would soon be declared.

21

Ravlos and Kareelya were watching Escoval on the viewing screen, and shaking their heads in disbelief at what they saw and heard.

Having safely neutralised the crystal by putting the wave deflector over it, the Doctor had switched on the screen to ensure that the way was clear for them to return to the laboratory. Instead of finding the way clear – they discovered treachery beyond their wildest imagining.

Escoval was breaking the cardinal rule.

Members of the Family never lied.

So it was almost with sadness that Ravlos spoke, as they watched the guards taking the blank-faced Shankel and his fellow-guard away.

'So – now we see the truth of the matter. Escoval is indeed a warmongering traitor, and also undoubtedly was responsible for smashing our equipment and putting our researches back, maybe by months.'

There was no sadness in Kareelya's voice when she spoke, only sheer amazement at the stupidity of Escoval's action. 'But why? What possible good can he achieve by putting Tranquela at risk of war with Ameliera like this? For all we know it may not be they who are responsible for what has been happening.'

The Doctor spoke quite softly as he continued to watch the screen intently. 'I would say undoubtedly *not* Ameliera. But if Escoval has his way, war *will* be declared, and your fellow-continent will soon be attacked.'

Ravlos was appalled at the thought and his words

succinctly explained the reason why. 'But they won't be expecting it – thousands of innocent people will die. The Armouries of both countries contain weapons of unbelievable ferocity.'

The Doctor viewed the screen for a few seconds more before turning to look at Ravlos, to whom he spoke in a voice almost tinged with jollity. 'Then we must go and warn them – mustn't we.'

Kareelya blurted out the remark before she could stop hereslf. 'No! Not us! Our presence would be a breach of the truce!'

Then she realised how sharply she had spoken. 'Sorry, Doctor.'

'No harm in speaking one's mind Kareelya – no harm at all.'

Ravlos clarified the position with a few well-chosen words. 'Kareelya is right. Our presence could indeed start the war we are trying to avoid.'

The Doctor responded yet again in the same cheery mood. 'Then it would indeed be rather foolish for you both to travel with me.'

'True,' said Ravlos, and then continued, 'We must stay here – try to clear our good name. Convince Abatan of the truth of the matter – that Escoval is a traitor.'

Kareelya knew she was asking a lot of their recently arrived friend, but she asked in any case. 'Will you carry the message to them, Doctor?'

He had no hesitation whatever. 'But of course. I trust these Amelierons are a reasonably understanding sort of a bunch? Not the sort who might pop me into a pot and boil me up for supper or any such?'

Ravlos and Kareelya exchanged a glance that didn't escape the Doctor. 'Ah – I see. You mean they *might* just pop me into a pot for supper.'

It was Kareelya who explained the glance they had exchanged. 'We quite simply have no idea, Doctor.'

Ravlos took up the story. 'All communication was severed after the pact, that was one of the agreements the pact contained, so we simply don't know how their culture has developed over the last fifty years or so.'

The Doctor mused on it, and then having given a thoughtful, 'Ah.' He continued, 'Any hints as to the way their culture was likely to go before the parting of the ways?'

Ravlos shook his head regretfully. 'I was only a young boy at the time of the separation.'

Kareelya remembered a detail that might have a bearing. 'They were a very religious people, I seem to recall; with an advanced awareness of "good".'

Ravlos was pleased at the thought. 'Chances are they'll still be a peaceful race then?'

Kareelya nodded her head in agreement.

The Doctor looked quietly relieved; he felt he had had enough excitement for one 'holiday' already.

'Oh - good - that's nice to know.'

If only he had known how obsessed the Amelierons had become in their mania for total goodness - he might not have been quite so nonchalant. But now he looked back to the screen, and his muttered, 'Ah,' made Ravlos and Kareelya also look in that direction.

Abatan had approached the TARDIS and was looking at it coldly as if he could see right through it. His command rang out clearly in the TARDIS. 'Break down its doors.'

As the guards moved forward, the Doctor could only smile at the idea. 'They haven't got a chance of succeeding.'

In the bare cells centred in the luxury of Abatan's state room, Peri and Locas sat, glum.

They had talked the subject of their captivity around and around to the point that there was nothing else to be said about it. Now they simply sat and waited to see what fate would finally bring them.

They didn't have long to wait.

In the distance they heard the noise of troops approaching, and soon the guard detail entered into the chamber with Shankel and the other zombie of a guard under close arrest.

Locas leaped to his feet and, rushing to the front of the cell he gripped the bars tightly. In his utter amazement he said just one word, 'Shankel!'

But Shankel didn't react to the name at all. It was as if he had never heard it before. He simply went on staring blankly ahead as he was led unprotesting, with the other guard, into the right-hand cell.

Peri had come to join Locas at the bars, seeing from the look of horror on his face that there was something deeply wrong.

She asked the question quietly. 'Who is he?'

Locas spoke in a voice that was tinged in disbelief as to what he was seeing happening. 'It is my friend Shankel. The one who I was taking you to meet at the Armoury. But...'

He crossed to the side bars that gave him the clearest view of his friend, and what he saw appalled him. He spoke in a voice tinged with horror. 'There's something dreadfully wrong with him, and with the other one – almost as if they were... brain dead.'

Escoval had watched with mounting pleasure the unsuccessful attempts of the guards to force open the doors of the TARDIS.

He realised that he now had the perfect excuse for achieving what he most desired – the reopening of the Armoury. Even though he tried, he could not hide the sneer in his voice as he spoke. 'It is no use trying to open it by brute force, Abatan – you're obviously going to have to get a "Ray-Burner" from the Armoury. That will go through it like a knife through lard.'

There was an air of desperation in the voice of Abatan as he screamed his one-word reply. 'No!'

Suddenly he had understood that Escoval was indeed driving him into a corner from which there would be no escape.

And Escoval of course recognised the tone, and knew he had Abatan against the wall. His voice was again full of scorn, but this time he did not even try to hide it. 'What other answer is there, "First Family Leader"?'

Abatan flushed to hear his rank used as an insult, but held his tongue.

Escoval continued goading him. 'Are you simply going to stand by and let the traitors, your "trusted friends", Ravlos and Kareelya, just fly out of here with all their knowledge of our defence and Armoury, along with the Amelieron spy? Is that what you really intend?'

He let that sink in before he laid on the ultimate threat. 'What do you think the rest of the Families will make of it, Abatan?'

He knew that Escoval was right. If that happened, and Ravlos and Kareelya truly were traitors, his rule would indeed be finished. The loss of office would be no great burden, but the thought of a man of Escoval's character ruling his beloved homeland was truly unthinkable.

Finally, when he accepted that the guards were not going to be able to open the TARDIS by brute force alone, he was left with no other option than the option he hated even contemplating.

It looked, unless some miracle soon ensued, that the Tranquelan Armoury would have to be reopened.

Inside the TARDIS the Doctor had watched Ravlos and Kareelya viewing the screen and listening to the discussion that was taking place between Escoval and Abatan intently.

He sensed that there was more import to the exchange than he had appreciated.

It was apparently no longer simply about trying to force an entrance to the TARDIS. Greater issues were obviously at stake. But what were they?

When Ravlos spoke, after one quick glance at Kareelya to see in her eyes that she agreed with him, all was made clear. 'We must go now, Doctor. Escoval is very persuasive. Once the Armoury is opened the fifty-year truce is officially broken. It is easier then to go forward and attack Ameliera, just in case, than to wait for the attack to come from them.'

Kareelya took up the story with sorrow in her voice. 'You see the problem, Doctor? To get inside to us, they have to open the Armoury – and war would follow. We would perhaps be responsible for that war. And even if it cost our lives – we could not take on that burden.'

With that Ravlos took her hand tenderly, then looked once more at the Doctor. 'We will go now, Doctor – face our fate. And to you is left the task of warning the Amelierons of what may happen. Please do not fail us.'

There was still something niggling at the back of the Doctor's mind.

They were simply too despondent about their chance of surviving. He decided to clarify it. 'Surely, if you tell Abatan the truth of the situation – that Escoval is lying in his teeth – all should be all right. Yes?'

Kareelya's gentle smile at the preposterous situation was very poignant, and the Doctor realised even before she spoke that they were indeed probably going to their death.

'The only problem is, Doctor, the leaders of the Families physically cannot lie. That is their one major strength, instilled from birth. They quite simply never, ever lie.'

Ravlos let that knowledge sink in before taking it to its natural conclusion. 'But, as you clearly see – Escoval *is* lying. He somehow has recovered the ability to lie. What an incredibly powerful weapon he therefore has in his hands.'

Kareelya then stated the final truth. 'How do we, mere scientists, convince the Council of Families that one of their number, after thousands of years of Family rule unblemished by such a dishonourable achievement, is committing such an impossible offence?'

They let the Doctor consider the conundrum for a few seconds, but no answer was forthcoming. Ravlos made the request. 'Would you open the doors, Doctor?'

The Doctor nodded sadly, desperate to argue them

into escaping, but knowing it was not his place to interfere. 'But of course.'

He crossed to the control panel and energised the motor that would open the doors of the TARDIS, and send Ravlos and Kareelya to certain doom.

At that moment, in the laboratory, Abatan's lips formed to make the command that would send troops dashing to open the Armoury doors. He gathered his breath to cry out the order.

Escoval knew it. He had been watching Abatan's face as he deliberated, and sensed the moment of his greatest ambition was upon him, Abatan was going to give the command now!

But before he could speak the doors of the TARDIS flew open and Kareelya and Ravlos appeared on the step.

Escoval was furious beyond measure, but not too furious to know what he must do next.

As the doors opened the troops fell back a little way. All watched intently. And none saw that Escoval had slipped the hypno-gun from his pocket and on to his finger, fired twice with dreadful accuracy, spearing both Ravlos and Kareelya between the eyes with the gun's minuscule ray.

As the TARDIS disappeared, and the troops fell even further back with the surprise of its departure, he took advantage of the opportunity, and rushed forward to grab both Kareelya and Ravlos by their unresisting arms.

Looking them in the face one after the other to ensure their eyes were on him, he screamed at them in a pretence of anger, as he instilled in them his hypnotic command. 'Tell Abatan that everything I told him was true! You wrecked the laboratory! You had an Amelieron spy here! Ameliera is about to attack us and take us by surprise! You are their spies! Tell him this is true! Tell him – traitors!'

Abatan dashed forward to grab Escoval roughly, and

pull him away from his old friends Ravlos and Kareelya. 'No more, Escoval! I want to hear it from their lips, not from yours!'

Escoval once more smiled his smug smile – he knew the damage had been done. 'Suit yourself, Abatan – ask away.'

And that is what he did, gently. 'Is this true, Ravlos – Kareelya? Is this terrible thing that Escoval says true?'

There was a long pause. A pause that was so long that Escoval once again began to worry that the gun had not worked.

He need not have worried. When they spoke in unison they were condemning themselves to death. 'Yes – it is true.'

For a moment there was disbelief in Abatan's face. Then he realised the only thing that could be done in the face of such a confession. The country must be protected.

He spoke the words that had not been spoken since the days of his father's father. 'Open the Armoury! Alert all our forces! From this moment the truce is at an end; and we are at war with the Amelierons!'

And with a dismissive wave to indicate Ravlos and Kareelya he said to the nearest guard, 'Take the traitors to their cells.'

As Abatan left the chamber, Escoval simply stood and smiled with unrestrained joy at the sheer pleasure of his achievement.

He had managed to get the first world war in fifty years successfully under way.

22

Inside the TARDIS, unaware of the fact that Ravlos and Kareelya were now indeed in very deep trouble, the Doctor was well pleased with the performance of his sometimes recalcitrant vehicle.

Within seconds it settled down at the chosen destination in Ameliera without a whisper of a problem, and one word escaped the Doctor's lips, 'Perfect.'

He leant forward and switched on the viewing screen, and as it sprang into life, he gave a 'Humph' of surprise at what was in view.

Nothing.

Nothing but swirling mist, that is.

'Strange.' He checked the control panel, mumbling to himself as he did so. 'All appears to be in order. Correct settings, correct co-ordinates, but...'

He went on to flick the viewing screen through a range of colour changes. Infra red, to ochre, yellow, green, and finally back to standard; and still there was only mist to be seen. 'Nothing.'

He glanced at another dial. 'Well – atmosphere normal enough – better pop out and take a look.'

He pressed the control, and the door smoothly opened. He crossed to look out but all that was to be seen was the same swirling mist. A blank, impenetrable wall that cut his vision down to no more than half a metre.

Fingers of mist crept into the doorway, and in a moment his decision was made. 'Ah well. Nothing venture...'

He stepped through the doorway of the TARDIS into the blanket of enshrouding grey.

'... nothing gain.'

He closed the door behind him, and moved forward a few paces. Immediately the TARDIS was engulfed in grey and disappeared from his view. He moved further forward and glanced around. Wherever he looked he was faced by the same solid wall of all-embracing greyness. He thought he heard something and listened intently, his head cocked to one side as if to catch the slightest sound.

Out of the greyness, pinpricks of light were approaching. He turned around and discovered he was, as he had guessed he would be, surrounded by a circle of minuscule sparks of light, brightening as they moved ever closer. They progressed through the mist, until he could see that the light was coming from tiny cones of glass sitting on top of thin glass barrels.

They were almost resting against the Doctor before he could confirm that the glass barrels were indeed guns.

The guns were held by humanoid individuals dressed in white boiler suits, their faces obscured by glass-domed helmets that allowed no view to the interior.

When all were in position around the Doctor, each gun just a fraction away from him in a perfect circle, they stopped.

The long silence that then held was finally broken by the Doctor himself, speaking at his cheeriest. 'How nice of you all to come and greet me like this.'

In the state room of Abatan, Peri and Locas were again standing at the bars of their centre cell.

This time they were watching as guards put Ravlos and Kareelya in the last vacant cell, to the left of them. They were just as blank-eyed as Shankel and the other guard who still sat in a daze at that very moment.

In the distance voices could be heard issuing urgent orders, and feet could be heard running to obey. Locas wondered what could be afoot to cause so much furore.

Ravlos and Kareelya being safely in the cell, the guards withdrew, locking the door behind them.

Locas's voice was horror-struck as he spoke. 'Look at them, Peri! Exactly the same as Shankel and the other guard.'

She had seen as much, and now asked the obvious question. 'But what is it? What's wrong with them?'

Locas shook his head, puzzled. 'I just don't know...'

The noise in the corridor grew in intensity, and Locas swung his head round to look in that direction. 'Listen!'

They both strained to hear what was being shouted by the guards, but could not make out the words.

In a sudden fury Locas went from the front bars where he stood, and crossed to the bars that divided their cell from the cell that Shankel was in. Quite harshly he grabbed Shankel by the hair and dragged him closer to the bars that separated them.

'Shankel! Shankel!! Speak to me!'

There was no reaction.

Locas put his other hand through the bars and slapped Shankel back and forth across the face to get some life back into him. 'Speak to me!'

Finally Shankel spoke, in the voice of an automaton, stilted and slow... 'Escoval is right. Ravlos and Kareelya were smashing equipment; an Amelieron spy who was with them struck us both down.'

Locas and Peri exchanged a glance, and then Locas couldn't stop himself exclaiming. 'That's crazy! Why on earth would Ravlos and Kareelya do anything so stupid?!'

But Peri had had a sudden thought. 'Ask him to describe the spy, Locas!'

'Why?'

Peri wasn't ready to reveal her reason yet. 'It's just a hunch – ask him.'

Locas leant closer to the bars. 'Tell us what this Amelieron spy looked like, Shankel.'

There was a long pause before Shankel spoke – but when he did there was no doubt at all in Peri's mind as to whom he was describing.

'Blond curly hair – grey eyes – a coat of many

colours...'

'I thought as much – it's the Doctor without a doubt!' interrupted Peri.

Locas let go of Shankel, who slumped back in his seat, and crossed to the cell that housed Ravlos and Kareelya. 'Ravlos! Ravlos! It's me, Locas. Tell me what happened to you!'

He paused hopefully, but no reply was forthcoming.

Then a look of determination came over Locas's face and he closed his eyes tightly, concentrated, and disappeared.

Before Peri had had time to recover from the surprise of his disappearance, he had materialised in the left-hand cell and was leaning over Ravlos and talking to him urgently. 'Ravlos! What is wrong with you?!'

No reply. Locas took him and shook him none too gently by the shoulders, repeating the question as he did so. 'Ravlos! Tell me what is wrong with you!'

And finally, and very mechanically, Ravlos spoke. 'Escoval tells the truth. We wrecked the laboratory. There was an Amelieron spy here called the Doctor. We are spies as well. Amelierons are about to attack Tranquela.'

Locas straightened up, aghast. Closed his eyes, shimmered, disappeared, and then reappeared once more standing beside Peri, looking deeply troubled.

'What does this mean, Locas? We know the Doctor's not an Amelieron – they know it as well. And they can't really be spies, can they?'

Locas's answer came without hesitation. 'No – impossible. But it is not Ravlos speaking.'

Peri couldn't stop the surprised exclamation. 'What!'

'I'm sure that Escoval has somehow managed to take over their minds – and the minds of Shankel and the other guard.'

As Peri took this in, he continued. 'If they all lie on his behalf – it can only mean one thing. He has broken the cardinal rule of the Families by *lying*, himself.'

'Is that bad?'

'Unforgivable. I further think that the noise we can hear in the corridor indicates that Escoval had also finally had his way; I believe that war with the Amelierons is probably imminent.'

'But surely from what you say your father would never allow that.'

Locas shook his head sadly. 'My father would never believe that Escoval could lie – therefore if he is deceived convincingly enough, he might well think he had no other option to save Tranquela, but by going to war with Ameliera.'

Suddenly Peri knew the only sensible thing they could do. 'We've got to get out of here and find the Doctor. He's the only one who's going to sort this mess out.'

But she had not reckoned on Locas's deeply ingrained sense of tradition. 'I can't, Peri. Family honour forbids it.'

The answer came spontaneously to her lips. 'What's family honour compared to the life of your whole planet – you tell me that, Locas?'

And she saw that she had won her point.

The grey of the Amelieron mist was an unbroken blanket. Suddenly, through the mist a figure appeared. He was surrounded by pinpricks of light, and the lights were seen to be guns, and the guns were held by white-clothed, faceless figures.

Having reached a certain point the figures indicated the Doctor should stop. No words had been exchanged, he simply knew they wanted him to stop.

So he stopped.

All those that had guarded him moved slowly backwards, disappearing one by one into the embracing arms of the mist, the last sight being the pinpricks of light. They too finally vanished and the Doctor was left standing alone, wondering what was to happen next.

A sucking noise was heard, not unlike the sound made by a large vacuum cleaner. At ground level all around the Doctor, at a distance of a few metres, the mist started to disappear into vents. It was sucked away so efficiently that in no time at all, all vestiges of its presence were gone, and the Doctor was left standing in what turned out to be a clinically clean, blindingly white room.

He looked around in his usual interested fashion and took note of the fact that there was no furniture save a white plasticised table with two moulded armchairs to either side of it.

There were no windows, and the source of light could not be seen, but it was everywhere, and very bright. He also noted that there was no obvious door to the room.

The Doctor, having seen enough, spoke his thought out loud for the benefit of anyone who might be listening. 'Dentist's waiting-room perhaps?'

The voice when it came was deep and well modulated, but having no hint of friendship or welcome in it whatever.

'You may be seated, intruder.'

The Doctor looked around to see if he could pinpoint where the voice was emanating from, but failed to do so. 'I'll stand, if it's all the same to you.'

There was a click, and from the walls projected thin nozzles, covering every possible line of fire in the room.

'You will sit or be evaporated – the choice is yours. You have ten seconds to decide. One, two, three, four...'

The Doctor spoke nonchalantly enough. 'Feet are feeling a bit tired, now you come to mention it.'

But the voice was counting on. '... Five, six...'

The Doctor was slowly strolling to the white table at the room's centre. 'Probably as well if I gave them a bit of a rest.'

Remorselessly the numbers kept coming. '... Seven, eight, nine...'

At which point the Doctor reached the table and sat on one of the chairs. 'Mm – quite comfortable as it happens.'

The voice stopped counting as the Doctor sat.

There was a short pause and the barrels smoothly

withdrew – the wall was matt white and flat once more.

The Doctor was just feeling the smoothness of the chair's arms when two hoops of strong white flexible material flicked out from under the arms to pinion his wrists tightly. As he struggled to get free his legs became level with the front legs of the chair, and two further bands snaked out from there and wrapped themselves around his ankles.

Realising his struggles were in vain he stopped, and waited to see what was in store for him next.

A humming noise was heard, and a section of the white wall started to slide aside.

If the Doctor had thought the light in the room was bright, he now knew that he had been overestimating its qualities. The light that shafted through the opening was painful in its intensity.

The Doctor closed his eyes, trying to blot it out, but it burned on even through the closed lids.

A tall thin figure of a man walked through the light and entered the room. He was wearing an all-white suit, as had the others, and he also wore a concave glass visor, through which nothing of his face could be seen.

As he paused menacingly at the doorway, the section of wall closed behind him, and the lighting diminished to its former level.

The Doctor finally opened his eyes. Saw the figure in front of him. And said the only thing that seemed to fit the occasion.

'Good evening! How nice of you to drop in!'

23

Escoval was in the Armoury corridor watching the frenzied activity of the troops with unrestrained joy.

Armament that had not seen the light of day for over fifty years was being brought out of storage looking as good as new.

The storing away had been executed by his grandfather, who had told him at his knee what he done to ensure that it would not deteriorate.

And now, as powerful-looking weapons were brought out in ever-increasing loads, Escoval knew that Grandad had truly done his work well.

Soon he would win the battle. And with Mordant's help he would also soon rule Tranquela.

Finally, satisfied with what he had seen, he turned and walked away.

Having greeted the white-clad stranger the Doctor said no more. He simply waited to see what would develop next. The figure crossed to sit in the chair opposite him. A long pause ensued which was finally broken by the Doctor. 'Weather a bit inclement for this time of year?'

The figure put his hands under the arms of his chair and pulled a thin cable from each. Each cable had a miniature cuff on the end.

The Doctor chatted on cheerily. 'Might come on to rain later if the mists don't let up.'

The figure clipped the cuffs around the Doctor's wrists just in front of the plastic hoops that already held his hands in an iron grip. Having done that he rested his arms back on his own chair.

The Doctor sensed it might be dangerous, but he could not resist one final comment. 'Of course - might be snow rather than...'

He had sensed rightly. As the Doctor spoke the figure simply pressed down on the arms of the chair, and the Doctor was immediately racked by unbelievable pain as an electric current was delivered through the thin cuff. He screamed then, and the pain was gone.

The Doctor was left drained.

When the man spoke again there was menace in his voice. And he made it chillingly clear what the threat was. 'Enough of the flippancy. You are here on trial for your life.'

In the cell Peri was still trying to get Locas to see the sense of what she was suggesting. 'You must do it, Locas! Your country depends on it. You said it yourself! Obviously your father's been taken in by Escoval's lies - simply because he knows it's impossible that anyone of the Families *could* lie. You've got to get us to the Doctor now!'

Finally common sense prevailed.

He agreed. 'You're right! If I'm to die in any case - better to die trying to stop Escoval's plans.'

Peri was overjoyed. 'Great! Now what?!'

Locas thought momentarily and then he had it. 'Tell me what I would have to "picture" to be sure to arrive with this Doctor of yours?'

A moment's thought and Peri knew. 'Well - the TARDIS I suppose.'

'The TARDIS?'

'The ship he travels in. It looks like an old British police box.'

'British? Police box?'

Peri saw that it might be slightly more difficult that she had anticipated. Then she had the perfect idea. 'No! Tell you what - imagine a round crystal like this.'

She indicated the shape of the holiday ball. 'Got it?'

Locas nodded his head.

'Good. The Doctor's got one in the TARDIS, and there couldn't be another like it within light years of this place.'

Now there was no further hesitation. Locas was as eager to be under way as Peri was.

'Right. A large crystal it is then.'

He opened his arms, Peri crossed to where he stood, he folded his arms tightly around her, they both closed their eyes. Shimmered.

And the centre cell was empty.

Mordant was so ecstatic with the news that Escoval was bringing him via the transponder screen that he hadn't even noticed he was drooling uncontrollably. He simply sat at the control panel with a euphoric smile on his ugly face, ignoring the dribble.

Escoval finally got to the point, and gave him the news he was longing to hear. 'So very shortly the first missiles will be launched!'

Said Escoval.

Mordant gave a 'Yarrow!' of joy, with such intensity that the bird was instantly awake and squawking!

It looked in Mordant's direction and started shouting. 'You're drooling again! You're drooling again!'

Mordant's tongue unrolled on automatic pilot and scooped up the gob while at the same time he grabbed a convenient crystal to throw at the cage, sending it swinging, and the bird screamed even louder.

At the same time he managed to carry on shouting his joyous thanks to Escoval. 'Excellent news, Escoval! I shall hold back on the hate beam this session – and reposition it so that the Amelierons can be washed with fear; that way the battle will be over very quickly. And then all that remains...'

But he was interrupted by the raucous alarm bell that forewarned him that his ship was being entered.

As a whirling apparition started materialising just to one side of the control desk in the cabin, he flung himself backwards, pressing the button to open his bolthole in the wall and screaming, 'Escoval! I am being invaded!!'

He dived into it, and the round steel shutter closed behind him. Escoval switched off and disappeared from the screen, by which time Peri and Locas had arrived safely - at the wrong destination.

Locas, opening his eyes, first caught a glimpse of the disappearing Mordant and exclaimed, 'What was that?'

Peri had more important things on her mind. 'Never mind what it was - we're in the wrong place!'

Locas picked up the crystal that Mordant had thrown at the bird, then saw the others lined up on top of the control panel. He pointed at them. 'Look.'

She looked at them, then took the one he was holding. 'They're the same crystals all right - but this most definitely isn't the TARDIS.'

She put the one she was holding down again. 'Just think of just one crystal exactly like that in the centre of a...' She fought for the apt words. 'A large squarish box? Yes that's it, that should get us there nicely. Ready?'

He indicated that he was ready by opening his arms. Peri joined him, and once he had her held tightly, they closed their eyes, shimmered, and disappeared.

The alarm bells, that had been ringing all the while in the background, stopped.

There was the slightest of pauses, then the steel shutter covering the porthole in the wall slid aside and Mordant popped his head out. Once he was sure that the coast was clear, he climbed out muttering to himself darkly as he once more crossed to the control panel.

'Is there no privacy left on this planet?!'

24

The Doctor's face was drained of colour.

He had lost track of how many times the electric shock had been administered, as his inquisitor tried to crush his spirit with the high-voltage charge delivered through the cuffs on his wrists.

His white-suited tormentor was now speaking of the Doctor with utter contempt, the disgust he felt apparent in his voice.

The Doctor listened carefully, knowing that this statement could provide the key to the mentality of the Amelieron race.

There was a trace of horror also present in the voice as he spoke on. 'The mists have deodorised you, sanitised you, bacteriolised you, but still you are unclean. What sort of race are you Tranquelans to come before us naked in this fashion?'

The word 'naked' fascinated the Doctor. He was dressed, therefore there was another Amelieron definition of the word that he must seek out.

'Laying aside for the moment the fact that I am not a Tranquelan – how can you say I'm naked? I thought I was quite reasonably turned out considering the small difficulties I've been undergoing lately.'

He saw that the figure was about to apply pressure to the arms of his chair and administer yet another shock, and understood it was not what he said as much as the way he said it that was causing the anger.

He quickly tried to right the situation, before the electric charge could be administered.

'That wasn't flippancy as you may think from the

tone I delivered the words in, as is the way on my home planet, but genuine interest. How do you define – undressed?'

There was a pause as the man considered whether the Doctor spoke the truth. Having decided he probably did he released the arms of his chair and sat comfortably once more.

'You allow yourself to see without an Interceptor, to hear without an Interceptor, to speak without an Interceptor; you probably even *think* without an Interceptor.'

To understand what was being said the Doctor needed to have the phraseology translated. 'Interceptor?'

'Yes – Interceptor.'

He touched the helmet he was wearing to indicate to what he referred.

'This, like all other Interceptors in our world, is hooked into "Central Computer" where is held all knowledge of what is "Good" and what is "Bad".'

The voice had spoken with pride. And the Doctor knew he must tread warily.

'And what is the function of "Central Computer" in this affair?'

Again the pride was clear in the voice, and the Doctor realised it was almost messianic; he was speaking as if of a 'God'.

'It filters out all evil, whether visual, oral, or mental; and allows us to be totally pure. A punishment is automatically administered by "Central Computer" if self-generated evil in any form is allowed to persist in the mind of the wearer.'

The words escaped the Doctor's lips before he could stop them. 'Obviously not much good on human "pongs" if my presence is causing such a furore.'

The figure pressed the arms of the chair with such violence that obviously he had been deeply stung by the Doctor's tone.

The Doctor writhed in agony as the shock juddered

through his body. Finally the chair arms were released and the torture stopped.

The Doctor fell back drained. 'Be warned. I am capable of killing you with this little toy.'

Slowly the Doctor recovered to the point where he could speak. 'Wouldn't killing be considered an evil by your "Central Computer"?'

The answer came back without any hesitation. 'Certainly not. You are not a "person" by our or its standard – simply a "thing". And things can be killed without compunction. Now, why do you come to Ameliera, Tranquelan intruder? Surely you must know the price of breaking the truce?'

The Doctor hazarded a guess. 'Death?'

'Quite,' replied the figure. 'So why do you come here courting death, stranger?'

The Doctor took his time about replying; he was intent on not receiving any more jolts. Finally he spoke. 'As I said – I am not a Tranquelan as you appear to think, though some of my best friends are and I feel no shame for that. I travelled here on their behalf to bring you a warning.'

The man straightened up in his chair at the word. 'A warning?'

'Yes.' The Doctor continued. 'Owing to a slight misunderstanding and a massive injection of Machiavellian shenanigans, war has been declared by the Tranquelans. You are in fact – about to be attacked.'

There was a pause as the man took this in. Cocking his head to one side as if listening.

And then it dawned upon the Doctor that that was exactly what he was doing. He was letting 'Central Computer' consider the implications and give him instructions as to his reaction.

Finally he straightened his head and spoke. 'Good.'

The Doctor was surprised at such a nonchalant reaction. 'Good?'

And then the reason was made crystal clear. 'Yes. I have consulted "Central Computer" and its judgement has been issued.

'If you are an example of the sort of creature that now inhabits Tranquela, then you all deserve to be destroyed.

'Our Armoury has been kept in good order. We would never of course attack and break the fifty-year truce. We are too honourable for such a course. But when attacked we shall repel, and then invade – and destroy.'

With that he put his hand back on the arm of his chair, and the Doctor braced himself for the shock.

But none was forthcoming.

All that happened was the cuffs around his wrists unlocked themselves, and flew back into their storage space under the arms of the opposite chair. Likewise the bands around his arms and legs sprang back into the hidden storage space from whence they had come.

The Doctor massaged his wrists and twirled his feet to get the circulation moving as the Amelieron continued talking.

'"Central Computer" has further decided that you shall be allowed to go free, and take the message back to the rest of your disgusting race. We shall fight this war and win. And soon every man and woman and child in Tranquela will have the ultimate privilage of being masked and under the care of "Central Computer".'

25

The TARDIS control area was empty of life. Suddenly, just to one side of the control panel itself, a whirlwind was seen to spin, and as it settled Peri and Locas appeared once more.

They opened their eyes in unison, and Peri gave a tiny scream of delight on realising they had made it. 'You've done it, Locas!'

He was a little perplexed. 'But where is this crystal you spoke of?'

Peri looked round and spied it under the glass helmet. She crossed to where the helmet stood, took it off the crystal, and stood it on one side, then picked up the crystal to show him. 'See. This is the one I was talking about.'

Then she put it back on to the control panel. But did not put the bowl back on it.

Inside his ship Mordant was delighted to see that once more the crystal had come back to life, and the scene in the TARDIS was again clearly in his view.

'Well, well, well. So we're back in contact with the dreadful Doctor, are we.'

As Peri and Locas spoke, he stroked the crystal to make their voices loud enough to hear without it being a strain and, once happy with the level, listened intently.

'But where is this Doctor?' said Locas.

'Good question,' agreed Mordant cheerily.

'Oh – I doubt whether he's far,' Peri replied.

'However far is not far enough young lady,' Mordant said tetchily.

Peri continued. 'Let's go and find him, shall we?'

Mordant had heard enough. He crossed to the control carrying the ball with him. Pressed a button and spoke tersely.

'Escoval! It's Mordant. Get up here. I want to talk to you about the final details of our deal now the battle is about to commence.'

With which he looked at the crystal and watched the disappearing backs of Peri and Locas.

'Go get him, children! Tell him Mordant awaits!'

And with that he burst into peal after peal of maniacal laughter.

Having walked through the TARDIS doors, and a few paces into the mist, Peri and Locas were engulfed in it. And lost. Peri grabbed Locas's arm. 'This is crazy! Let's go back to the TARDIS.'

Locas was agreeable enough. 'OK.'

But they set off back fractionally in the wrong direction, and the TARDIS wasn't where they expected.

Soon they were stumbling around blindly, desperately feeling for its comforting surface. It was nowhere to be found.

'Peri!' Locas called out sharply.

She stopped feeling for the TARDIS, her arms outstretched, and instead looked in the same direction as Locas.

Pinprick lights were approaching out of the gloom. The lights moved ever closer, until finally they were surrounded. They could distinguish that the lights were on guns, and that the guns were carried by masked figures dressed all over in white.

In their cell in the state room of Abatan, Ravlos and Kareelya were still befuddled, but slowly, very slowly, they were coming out of their hypno-gun-induced coma and back to their senses. In the far cell Shankel was also stirring into life.

Abatan and two guards walked into the chamber. All three were now armed. Abatan crossed to the centre cell purposefully, intent on having words with Locas. He stopped, horror-struck, in his tracks, when he saw the centre cell was empty.

When he spoke his voice was full of defeat. 'Oh, no Locas! How could you do such a thing? We shall never be able to lift our heads in Council again.'

Abatan turned and addressed the guards. 'Come. Let us to battle. My son has already taken the coward's route.'

As they turned to walk away, Ravlos gathered his strength and called out weakly. 'Wait, Abatan! I must tell you the truth before you go...'

Abatan turned to look at him and spoke coldly. 'Too late, Ravlos. You have already told the truth, old man; you are a traitor, by your own admission.'

Ravlos struggled to the front of the cell. As he spoke Kareelya sat up to listen. 'No! Only under the influence of Escoval! He pointed something at me as I came out of the ship. Some sort of hypno-gun I would imagine. I lied! As did Kareelya.'

And then, realising the enormity of what he was about to say, his voice fell almost to a whisper. 'Same as he, Escoval, lied.'

Abatan screamed his furious reply at such a major slur against a member of a Family. 'That is impossible! The Families cannot lie!'

There was a long pause before Ravlos could say the words. But he knew they must be said. 'I am afraid it is true.' He let that sink in before continuing with the catalogue of deceit.

'There was no Amelieron spy; only an old friend of ours called the Doctor. Escoval knew his name; and also knew he wasn't from Ameliera. But Escoval did the impossible. He lied about him.'

Shankel had by now managed to crawl to the bars of his cell. He spoke weakly.

'Escoval shot me and the guard with some sort of gun

also. He made us leave our post. We also lied.'

Abatan finally understood that they were both speaking the truth. His mind raced with thoughts of what must be done. In a flash he had it. 'We must stop the conflict!'

Kareelya called from the back of the cell, where she had by now recovered enough to have taken in all the previous discussion. 'It is too late, Abatan. The Doctor went to warn the Amelierons – now they too will be preparing to attack, in their own defence.'

Slowly the full reality of what was afoot hit Abatan. He shook his head sadly. 'This is madness. Sheer madness. And Escoval shall pay with his life.'

The same moment that Abatan spoke, the gun on the surface of Mordant's planetoid ship swung in an arc, until finally it was directed at its new target, Ameliera.

And the electrons dancing in the barrel of the gun, waiting to be released, slowly changed colour from a deep and burning maroon to a perfect, buttercup yellow.

No word was spoken by the figures surrounding Peri and Locas; they simply continued to menace them with their guns.

Peri wondered what was to happen next. In her wildest imaginings she would not have come to the right answer.

The Doctor came marching out of the mist through the circle of gunmen, pushing any barrels that got in his path nonchalantly out of the way.

When he finally reached the amazed Peri his greeting was the usual cheery remark, 'Ah, Peri. How nice of you to drop in and see me like this. And who's the young chap you've brought along with you?'

She could not believe it. 'Is that all you've got to say? The last time you saw me I was a guaranteed "goner", about to be stoned to death.'

'True,' said the Doctor jovially. 'But as you're not "gone" it obviously worked itself out in the end so we needn't waste our time chattering on about it.'

She was lost for a reply, a fact the Doctor noted with satisfaction, and he carried on talking in the face of it. 'There are of course much more important things to be done – so let's get the introductions of the way, then be on our way.'

Peri did exactly that. 'Locas – meet the Doctor.'

Locas smiled a greeting. 'Hello.'

The Doctor took his hand and shook it briefly.

'Delighted I'm sure. Right – off we go.'

Peri waved at the guards still surrounding them in tight formation. 'What about this lot?'

The Doctor looked around trying to work out to whom she referred. 'This lot?!'

And then he had it. 'Oh, that lot. They're all right – sort of escort I think – be glad to see the back of us. We apparently possess a somewhat putrid pong – spiritually speaking, that is.'

Peri was suitably irate at the thought. 'I'd prefer you spoke for yourself, thank you very much.'

'Don't blame me,' said the Doctor. 'Address your complaint to "Central Computer".'

And then he turned to talk in a friendly fashion to those who surrounded them. 'Right chaps. Like to lead us back to our motor?'

26

Inside his ship, Mordant watched Escoval poring over the documentation that he had handed him as soon as he arrived, with extreme interest.

This was the moment that the Salakans loved. The signing of the first contract. Once this piece of paper was signed, the planet was as good as theirs.

The paperwork was always passed to any given client at the precise moment of maximum stress. Just when the client was in sight of what he thought was to be his victory, in fact. The client usually signed it with barely a glance.

Escoval was different. He finally stopped reading and looked up. 'But there's no term to this agreement?'

Though somewhat surprised at Escoval's astuteness in noticing the point, considering the stress he was under, Mordant wasn't to be thrown. 'Of course there's no term to it. Once war is re-established, it'll never go away. You'll need new and ever more sophisticated weapons every couple of years at least, plus some way of keeping your enemies... content. Why put a term to it when it'll obviously be an ongoing situation?'

Escoval's face hardened at the thought. 'I can't agree to that.'

There was a choice available to Mordant: he could cajole or threaten. He decided to threaten.

'That's all right. I'll turn the fear ray on your troops instead of on the Amelieron troops. If you think my hate gun was strong – you should see what naked fear does to a man. And that's what it's programmed to send at the moment. Your men would flee the battle in seconds –

screaming, same as the Amelierons are going to do – providing I direct it at them, that is.'

It was as if Escoval were seeing Mordant for the first time. 'You are a hard man, Mordant.'

Mordant smiled, pleased at the thought. And then he played his trump card, Escoval's ambition. 'Do you want to rule this planet or don't you? It is as simple as that.'

Escoval considered the point momentarily. And the answer was that of course he did. He bent over and signed the first contract with a flourish.

Mordant said just one word. 'Good.' Then he took the paper from Escoval, rolled it up and crossed to the panel. 'And now, let me show you what my little gun can produce in the way of fear. The gun is directed at Ameliera now, so your troops are quite safe.'

He went to turn a switch, and as he did so noticed that the Doctor was once more on the crystal in the TARDIS.

'So – the Doctor is back on the TARDIS once more; who better to demonstrate the power of the fear wave. Now I'll make him dance for you.'

He was about to flood the TARDIS with fear via the crystal when Escoval's cry stopped him. 'No! Let us wait, listen, and see what he has discovered!'

The Doctor had stopped in the middle of the cabin and was looking intently at Peri.

She had just told him of their strange adventure whilst trying to rejoin him and the TARDIS. Hearing the story of the man fleeing into a secret compartment in the ship's wall was what had fascinated him.

'And what did this little man look like?'

'Hard to say. We only caught a glimpse of him as he disappeared into this "porthole" thing like an agitated monkey.'

Locas added his memory of the incident. 'Small and ugly would just about sum him up from what I saw.'

And now the Doctor knew who it most likely was. 'Dwarf Mordant to a "T". I thought as much. All we've got to do now is to find out where the drooling little toad is, and this business will be settled in no time.'

And with that, to Locas and Peri's amazement, the Doctor was racing across the TARDIS heading for the crystal on the control panel. Not knowing that Mordant at the same second, having first screamed at Escoval, 'He's going to put the bowl back on the transmitter!', was also running, intent on pressing the button that would make the Doctor his slave once more.

Luckily, the Doctor got there first, and in a flash the deflector bowl was safely back on the crystal making it harmless once more, with the Doctor left standing there panting.

When he had finally recovered his breath he looked to Peri and chided her. 'Peri. How many times do I have to tell you? Don't interfere with things that don't concern you.'

The answer came in a flash. 'Obviously a few more times yet, Doctor.'

And then she gave him her friendliest smile. 'Good to be back.'

When Escoval finally got bored with Mordant kicking the now dead crystal around the cabin, he interrupted with a question, 'So he escapes?'

Mordant stopped raging and thought about it. Then his face beamed with pleasure. He had the answer.

'Not quite. Being on Ameliera they're still in the path of the main beam of my gun. The setting is now to fear. Let's see how they like a touch of that particular nastiness.'

Having switched on the gun and heard it roar into life above his head, he turned back to Escoval. 'And now – to the other paperwork.'

Escoval was somewhat surprised. 'But we've already signed the contract.'

'No no no,' said Mordant. 'That was only the document of intent – now we get down to the main detail and the paperwork proper.'

With which he brought out a stack of contracts

already filled in and ready for signing. 'Get on with it, shall we?'

Mordant did not give a further thought to the Doctor and those on the TARDIS – he knew that resisting the fear ray was hopeless, and that they would be under its power until he chose to switch it off.

He was right.

On the TARDIS the effect was traumatic beyond imagining. Being in the direct line of fire, Peri was the first one the fear washed over, closely followed by Locas.

Terrified, they clutched each other for comfort, but only momentarily.

Peri suddenly became the object of Locas's fear. She was the most terrifying person in the world. Locas broke free with a scream and ran to hide in a corner as far away from her as possible. Curling up into a tight foetal ball that he hoped would make it impossible for her or anybody else to attack him, his teeth chattering uncontrollably, he sat and simply sobbed.

Peri was totally uninterested in Locas's problems, for she had seen the Doctor and he had become the focus of her terror. He was now a grotesque monster. Every being that she had ever been afraid of as a child was seen in his face. He changed from one to the other before her eyes. She ran away to another corner as far away from him and Locas as possible, crying and shouting, 'Don't hurt me, bogey man! Please don't hurt me!'

And as for the Doctor?

He had simply slumped down at the control desk shaking from head to toe, and looking at the panel which suddenly started to writhe before his eyes, undulating like a snake, until finally it started to crawl with life.

Various toggle switches and handles on the control panel had taken on a life of their own. Every crawling creature that man had ever feared was there. Spiders, snakes, toads, centipedes, rats – all were present, and all were looking at the Doctor malevolently; he could clearly see the desire they had to kill him.

27

Mordant was checking the viewing screen. Flicking from place to place, he dropped in on various parts of Ameliera.

Wherever he looked he saw the same thing – white-uniformed figures clutching at their helmets which overheated as Central Computer tried, and failed, to keep the fear that was flooding in under control.

As each helmet failed its wearer fell to the ground, writhing with terror.

Well pleased with what he had seen, Mordant turned to look at Escoval who was just signing the last few papers. 'Good. The Doctor will be well taken care of; and by the look of it, the Amelierons won't be retaliating at all when the attack is under way.'

Escoval crossed to him and gave him the papers, looking at the screen as he did so. 'That will be as soon as I return – they look ready to surrender without a shot being fired.'

'Quite,' said Mordant. Then he looked at Escoval, appraising him. 'So, Escoval – your victory will be assured. And to you is then left the small task of removing Abatan and taking the rule yourself. Do you think you'll be capable of doing so?'

Escoval was smugly confident. 'It should present no difficulty. It is after all in my blood. In fact, being honest, it will be a pleasure. For years my family have suffered under his patronising First Family posturing – now I'll go and kill him, and delight in the task.'

With which he closed his eyes ready to transport himself out of the ship.

But Mordant's cry stopped him in his tracks. 'Not so fast, Escoval! There is one last paper to be signed.'

Escoval opened his eyes. Now they were hooded with displeasure. He was hungry to get the war under way and over with, so he could exercise the joy of power. His voice was cold and quite threatening when he finally spoke. 'One more?'

Mordant saw that he was pushing Escoval's patience to the utmost. But that was no bad thing. The angrier he was the quicker he would sign what was put in front of him to get it over with.

Mordant spoke at his crawlingly sycophantic best. 'We Salakans like to make sure that all the people we... help... on various planets are quite aware of the finer details of the various contracts, and what their part in the bargain must be before we help complete the destruction of their enemy. We now have the future trade contract to consider.'

'Future trade?' It was obviously the first that Escoval had heard of this particular item.

'Yes. You will have a new continent in your control – but how to control your new continent, and keep them happy, is of great importance to us.'

Escoval brightened. 'You have a... substance?'

'We have a substance. It's not cheap – but there again guaranteed peace never is. Also we have mining contracts on other worlds where your prisoners, the Amelierons, could earn the exchequer much-needed financing.'

Escoval smiled at the wealth of 'goodies' that Mordant and his countrymen, the Salakans, had on offer. 'Then let us talk.'

The Doctor was fighting one of the greatest battles of his life. Peri and Locas were too locked in their own terror to be even aware of his. He knew there was only one way out of the predicament that they were in. He had guessed quite correctly that he was being washed by some version of generated emotion. And as Mordant had used hate on the Tranquelans, common sense dictated that the Amelierons could be weakened and best prepared for battle by being washed by fear.

It took no great leap of the imagination to come to the conclusion that if he could get away from the continent of Ameliera, and out of the gun's rays, the problem would probably disappear. He closed his eyes to hide the monstrous writhing of the control panel. As the mouths of the tiny monsters still gnashed their teeth at him in his mind's eye, he spoke to himself through lips and jaws clenched tight against the nightmare that was filling his brain. 'Must try to control it. Must try to move out of its path.'

Eyes still closed, he struggled to stand, and having been driven to his knees once by the weight of his fear, he finally managed it. He knew that if he opened his eyes he would be lost. So, instead, he started to set the controls by touch alone.

They still writhed underneath his hands. Instead of feeling solid steel and plastic, he was feeling soft furry creatures that wriggled as he touched them, and the scaled and slimy bodies of snakes and cockroaches were also there.

He started to feel that they were crawling up his arms under his jacket sleeves, nipping him as they went; but he didn't give up on his task. Even though he longed to scream to get away from the tension and pain of it, he persisted.

Finally, when he felt the course was set, he opened his eyes and looked for the starting button; and there it was in front of him.

Trouble was – it was nestling at the back of the throat of a giant ferret. The ferret's mouth was wide open. Its razor-sharp teeth were held ready to bite down hard and inflict a cruel wound if the Doctor even dared to put his hand in its throat to press the button. But, closing his eyes once more, that is exactly what the Doctor did. As expected no wound was inflicted, and the TARDIS sprang into life, the lights dimmed momentarily, and the journey, no sooner started, was over.

The ship was now out of the fear zone, and the madness was behind them.

Peri and Locas shook the last vestiges of horror out of their minds, stood and crossed groggily to where the Doctor calmly checked the position they had arrived at. 'Good. Safe in a different time layer.'

Peri got enough control to ask the question. 'What was all that about?!'

The Doctor was now moving purposefully, and spoke as he did so. 'Fear, I would imagine. Simply fear. But a mighty weapon indeed.'

He was soon at the storage locker and searching for the object he required.

Peri was there at his shoulder, questioning him further. 'Fear?'

He searched on as he spoke. 'Take every fear that man is heir to – agoraphobia, zenophobia, vertigo; whatever you will – put them in a pot and stir them up together and that's what you get. Naked fear.'

Peri was horrified at the thought. 'But who would do such a thing?'

The Doctor had found what he was searching for. The square box with leads attached that he had shown Peri the day before. He came out of the locker and closed the door behind him as he spoke. 'Dwarf Mordant would.'

Locas had joined them and he now asked the obvious. 'But why?'

The Doctor was crossing to the control panel and Peri and Locas followed. 'A very good question and one that I hope shortly to have the answer to.'

Peri was struck with another thought. 'Do you think it was just us that were affected?'

The Doctor looked at her and shook his head gravely. 'No. At a guess I'd say the whole continent of Amelieron. And, before you ask the question, I should imagine to make them too frightened to fight – but to save the guesswork we'll go and ask Mordant, shall we?'

And with that he started to attach the leads that

unfurled from the box as he pulled them, two to the helmet covering the crystal, and another two to the TARDIS's controls.

Locas watched what the Doctor was doing, fascinated. 'What is that thing, Doctor?'

'Care to explain, Peri?'

She thought a moment and then remembered. 'It's a "wave tracker" that the Doctor keeps in his junk cupboard.'

He looked at her and raised an eyebrow, but didn't make any comment.

Peri continued. 'The idea is if you attach it to the TARDIS's controls, and the source of the wave, it will take us right to the point of the wave's emanation.'

The Doctor, having finished attaching the leads, stood back happily to view his work as he spoke. 'Well remembered, Peri. And now...' he said switching on the TARDIS main engine. 'Let us beam ourselves along the crystal's path to arrive, as Peri so succinctly put it, at the very source of its emanation where, if I'm not very much mistaken, we shall find the dreadful Dwarf Mordant.'

28

Mordant was watching Escoval, who was reading the final and most complex of the agreements for the third time.

Finally he could not resist commenting. 'I said *read* the small print. Not try to memorise it.'

Escoval ignored the comment and went on slowly reading. Mordant was getting quietly irate. 'Just sign it, Escoval! Why all this mistrust?'

Escoval looked at him coolly. 'Because, as future ruler, I want to know exactly what I'm letting my planet in for.'

As he spoke, behind them, and unseen by either of them, the TARDIS started slowly materialising alongside the control panel. Having arrived along the path of the wave emanation, no alarm had been triggered.

And so it was, as Escoval bent to sign the final agreement, and Mordant smiled gleefully, the doors of the TARDIS slid open and Locas was there to see the deed being done.

His fury grew as he took in the scene, dwarf and traitor side by side.

Finally the tension was too great and he had to speak. His voice rang out clear and accusingly. 'Escoval! You are a traitor!'

At that both Mordant and Escoval swung round to see who spoke. Mordant, immediately he saw the presence of the TARDIS, the Doctor and the strangers standing in its doorway, pressed the button on the wall beside him. The panel having slid aside, he dived head first through, to disappear inside. The panel clanged shut behind him.

Escoval left equally quickly. He simply closed his eyes, shimmered, and was gone.

As he vanished Locas closed his eyes and also disappeared.

The Doctor and Peri were left in the cabin alone. He turned to Peri and spoke with feigned seriousness. 'Perhaps there's something in what the Amelierons say about our smell after all.'

Escoval re-materialised as he had planned, in an empty corridor around the corner from the Armoury. He took out the hypno-gun and held it at the ready, then started walking to the Armoury corridor.

At that moment Abatan came around the corner with two armed guards. They stopped in their tracks as they saw who was there, the very man they were searching for.

Seeing him, Abatan could not stop himself exclaiming furiously, 'Escoval! I have been searching for you! Ravlos and Kareelya are now free, as are the guards. You are a traitor, and perhaps, even worse, a *liar*!'

Before he could say another word Escoval lifted the hypno-gun and coolly shot the two guards between the eyes. They didn't even have time to lift their own guns before being turned into mindless automatons.

Escoval smiled and then gave the instruction to the guards calmly, pointing at Abatan as he did so. 'Kill him!'

As one, the guards turned their guns on Abatan.

At the same moment, further along the corridor behind Escoval, Locas appeared. 'Escoval! I'm going to kill you!'

Escoval swung around to face the unarmed Locas as shots rang out behind him.

Knowing that Abatan was now dead, and he had all the time in the world, he decided to make the most of it. He drew his hand gun very slowly against the unprotected Locas, rather hoping that he might try to de-materialise to escape his fate, then he could shoot him as he departed, and Locas would have arrived at his destination dead.

But Locas showed no sign of doing so.

After a pause Escoval finally spoke, spelling out his intent. 'Now your father is dead, Locas, you are the last remaining member of the hateful and over-proud First Family to be removed.'

He smiled and raised his gun into firing position. 'It is my pleasure to perform that simple task.'

It was at that moment that the voice of the 'dead' Abatan rang out, echoing loudly down the corridor. 'Not quite dead, Escoval!'

The guards, as commanded by Escoval, had indeed pulled their triggers to shoot Abatan at point-blank range. But their action, done against their will, and slowed by the effects of the hypno-gun, had been signalled to Abatan, who, at the very last second, jumped out of the line of fire.

The two guards, having accidentally shot each other, were lying on the floor of the corridor, mortally wounded.

On hearing the voice, Escoval swung round desperately, his face horror-struck with the shock of hearing Abatan speak, when he had known he must surely be dead.

Abatan did not hesitate.

As Escoval raised his gun to fire it was too late.

Abatan shot him dead.

Inside Dwarf Mordant's planetoid ship the Doctor hummed a little tune to himself as he waited for a reply from the wall that he had just sharply rapped with his knuckles.

As no reply was forthcoming, he knocked again, this time directly on the porthole of metal through which Mordant had fled, calling as he did so. 'Come out Mordant! I know you're in there!'

There was another long pause.

Peri was standing beside the Doctor and she asked the

obvious, 'Will he finally come out, do you think?'

'Oh yes,' said the Doctor. 'And he'll have some little surprise in store for us, I shouldn't wonder.'

And with that there was a deep rumble and the whole of the wall containing the porthole started to move aside.

Inside the revealed cubicle a massive black, steel-clad robot was to be seen. It was threatening in its immensity and as its eyes rolled into life and it moved forward with a roar, Peri gave a scream.

Then it stopped just in front of them and lifted its arms high above their heads, all ready to smash them down and club both of them to death.

In the corridor Abatan turned Escoval over with his foot.

Locas walked along the corridor to join him.

Abatan looked at him, and then said without expression, 'The traitor is dead. All that remains is to let the Amelierons know what has been going on here.'

He looked at Locas coolly, wondering if he would be brave enough to take on the task.

Locas did not disappoint him. He simply said, 'Leave it with me, Father.'

He closed his eyes, and disappeared from the corridor.

The robot's arms were still aloft when it gave a final roar.

Peri fell to her knees and rolled to one side to escape the blow, then she was on her feet and running for the TARDIS. 'Come on Doctor! Quickly!'

But getting to the doors she realised that she was by herself and that the Doctor hadn't even flinched.

Instead he did a thing that amazed her. Even though she was used to seeing the Doctor do unlikely things, this was quite staggering in its silliness.

As the robot stopped roaring the Doctor simply knocked loudly on the robot's steel breastplate as if he was knocking on somebody's front door. He spoke loudly and commandingly as he did so.

'Come on Mordant! I know you're in there. Get out here, we have things to discuss.'

There was the slightest of pauses, then the robot's breastplate slid aside, and Mordant's face appeared at the opening. 'Hello Doctor! What a nice surprise!'

And with that Mordant was climbing out of the hole and dropping to the floor. Mumbling to himself as he did so. 'Pity about that – it usually works.'

Peri came out of the doorway of the TARDIS and headed for where the Doctor and Mordant stood.

The Doctor was speaking to him quite gently as if to a naughty child who didn't really know any better.

'Now what *is* going on here, Mordant? Even by normal Salakan standards you're causing something of a kerfuffle on this innocent little planet. What's it all about?'

Mordant, having been spoken to like a child, started to behave like one. He dropped his head, held his hands behind his back and stood in front of the Doctor shifting from foot to foot as he explained.

'Always the same when it comes to the arms trade Doctor – I mean if they won't fight how are we going to move our weapons?'

'The arms trade?' said Peri in a voice tinged with horror.

Mordant looked at her with a face full of bravado. 'Yeh. What's it to you?'

And with that he crossed to the control panel and climbed up on to his seat to check that everything was in order.

The Doctor explained it to Peri. 'Among their many industries the Salakan production of arms is unmatched in the universe.'

Mordant, hearing the Doctor, could not resist throwing in the sulky comment, 'Oh yes. And we salesmen have our work cut out at the best of times to shift them all. But if a planet won't have wars it's disastrous. Still – now I've got this bunch sorted out it'll be a great help.'

With that he carried on adjusting the dials, while speaking aloud for his own benefit. 'Right – now I've got the Amelierons cowed with fear; just direct a bit of evil at the Tranquelans, and the war will be under way in a flash.'

The Doctor's one word cracked through the cabin with the force of a whip. 'Stop!'

Having momentarily frozen, Mordant turned and spoke in a voice full of amazement. 'Stop?'

The Doctor strolled over to the panel where Mordant was sitting. 'Yes. You're finished here, Mordant.'

The Doctor leant over and checked the possible calibrations on the emotion gun. 'Right. Change the setting to "Goodness and Peace" and bathe both continents in its glow.'

Mordant was beside himself with a combination of fury and disbelief. 'You've got to be joking?! They'd both reseal their Armouries! The war wouldn't even start!'

The Doctor nodded his head agreeably. 'Exactly.'
Mordant looked as though he was about to have an attack of apoplexy, jiggling angrily on his seat, and in great danger of falling off.

'You can't make me do such a despicable thing as spread peace, Doctor! It's unnatural!'

The Doctor smiled happily at him. 'Can't I now? Remember the Time Lord's golden rule, Mordant?'

And with that the Doctor indicated the ten crystal balls neatly lined up along the top of the control panel.

Mordant's face dropped as he realised what the Doctor meant. 'Oh dear! I was forgetting. You're right of course. Still – there are plenty more planets to go and work on, and I didn't think much of this one in any case.'

And with that he started resetting the gun's emotion control, speaking as he did so. 'Peace and goodness it is then. Yuk!'

Having reset the controls he turned to look at the

Doctor. 'There we go, Doctor. You want this to be a boring old peaceful planet, and that's exactly what you'll have now. Happy?'

'Happy enough for now. All that remains is to see you safely off the premises.'

'OK Doc, fair enough.' He indicated the TARDIS. 'If you shift the bus I'll be on my way.'

29

Watched by Locas and Abatan, the last of the weapons were going back into the Armoury, hopefully never again to see the light of day in their lifetime.

Locas turned and watched his father's tired face, the strain of the last few hours clearly etched there. Finally he touched his arm to attract his attention. Abatan turned to look at him.

There was a pause before Locas spoke. 'All forgiven, Father?'

There was a long pause before Abatan replied. 'There is no longer anything to forgive. Your bravery in going to see the leader of the Amelierons and asking that the truce be reinstated showed me you were no coward.'

Locas thought briefly of his recent trip into the mists of Ameliera to talk to their leader and then wiped it out of his mind. He had been more frightened than at any other time in his life, but it had had to be done if war was to be averted.

He concentrated once more on what his father was saying. 'I now understand you did all you did for the good of the planet. And now the Amelierons have agreed that the truce will continue – we are as we were before. Your friend the Doctor is at this moment seeing that the source of the madness is safely removed – so, peace once more will reign.'

As he spoke, the last of the weapons went inside and the doors of the Armoury swung closed with a satisfying clang.

Two soldiers took up positions of guard on either side, and the rest of the troops started making their way back to their quarters.

After a long pause Abatan spoke again, an air of weariness in his voice. 'When I am sure the war is truly over, and peace has truly returned, I will be free to break a vow that I made to an old friend, and let you into a secret, Locas.'

Locas turned to look at him, wondering exactly what the secret could be.

The TARDIS is suspended in space standing sentinel to a planetoid.

The planetoid has a gigantic telescopic gun on top of it.

Motors are heard to roar and the gun sinks out of sight into the bowels of the planetoid, to be replaced by a section that matches the rest of the surface exactly.

A long pause ensues, and then, with a roar, the planetoid is on its way, disappearing into the distance, to who knows where.

Mordant having gone, the war is truly at an end, and the Doctor and Peri are free to go about their business once more.

Inside the TARDIS the Doctor was yet again busy at the storage locker searching for something as Peri chatted on. 'But what I still don't understand, Doctor, is *why* your pointing at the crystals on the control panel should have changed his mind so quickly?'

The Doctor continued his search as he replied. 'He knows the golden rule.'

'The golden rule?'

The Doctor paused in his search to explain. 'The Time Lords have an unbending rule as to anybody convicted of spying on them.'

Peri started to get the gist of what Mordant had been up to. 'Those other crystals were spying on other Time Lords?!'

'The potential was there – yes.'

The Doctor searched on.

'And Mordant knew the punishment applicable. Hence his speed at agreeing to destroy the crystals and to forget his business on that particular planet.'

Peri had the feeling she might not like to know the answer, but asked the question in any case. 'And the punishment?'

The Doctor found what he was looking for, a dog-eared magazine. He brought it out of the cupboard and closed the door. 'Gene manipulation. Mordant's parents would have been sought out – and it would have been arranged that instead of this Mordant being born, another Mordant would have been born. Minus the desire to spy of course. Mordant knew that if that happened he'd never make it to be Salakan's top salesman which he undoubtedly is. So – better and safer simply to find another market-place.'

The Doctor blew the dust off the magazine, saying, 'Just what we need.'

And with that he headed back to the main cabin, Peri following. 'But what is it, Doctor?'

He smiled at her. 'A holiday brochure. I think we really could do with a holiday now.'

Peri was suitably pleased. 'Now that is a great idea!'

The Doctor started flicking through the magazine. 'Anywhere in particular you'd like to try?'

And in a flash Peri had it. 'How about Majorca?'

The Doctor smiled at the thought of her change of view.

'Good! One last message to Locas to let him know that Mordant has truly gone, and we'll be on our way.'

Locas went to his father in the state room to give him the message that he had just received from the Doctor and Peri.

It was truly at an end.

His father smiled, relieved, and came to him and took his hand.

When he spoke there was a softness in his voice that Locas had never heard before. 'We parents are funny when it comes to protecting our children. We try to save them from as much harm as we possibly can. So much so that sometimes our children get hurt.'

Locas was totally thrown by the conversation. He had never heard his father talk in such an emotional way. It seemed almost as if he was fighting tears.

'There was a father who didn't want to risk his child being hurt any further; so he made me promise I would not speak until the war was at an end, even though it cost me dear not to speak, because you were also being hurt.'

Locas remembered the cryptic remark his father had made earlier about some secret he had to reveal, and wondered if this was going to be it. He waited with bated breath to hear what was going to be said.

When it came it was a bombshell.

Abatan spoke it very quietly, almost in a whisper, as though he were afraid to say it aloud in case it turned out not to be true. What he said was—

'Mariana is not dead.'

Locas's head reeled with the impact of the news; he couldn't believe he had heard correctly. 'But Father, I saw her die.'

Abatan shook his head. 'You saw her fall, Locas.'

He let that sink in before he continued. 'As she fell, she closed her eyes, and thought of home, and the parents she loved. And that is where she safely transported. She was in a state of shock but safe.

'Some days later, when she finally recovered enough to speak, and her parents heard her story, she was banned from seeing you until the madness was over.

'Her father told me yesterday that she was alive – but swore me to secrecy.'

Abatan looked to a guard on the far side who stood by a small door that led to a courtyard beyond.

'Open the door,' Abatan called.

The door was opened, and into the chamber walked Mariana. Locas ran towards her screaming her name with joy.

Abatan and the guards simply watched with pleasure as the children fell into each other's arms, and embraced for the whole world to see.